# PRAISE FOR SUZANNE ELIZABETH'S AWARD-WINNING DESTINY SERIES

## DESTINED TO LOVE

"The most delicious, thrilling, rambunctious time-travel adventure to come along in a long time."

—*Romantic Times*

"Suzanne Elizabeth manages to yet again breathe an air of freshness and life into the genre. *Destined to Love* is poignant, and compellingly unforgettable."

—*The Talisman*

## DESTINY AWAITS

"Funny, enchanting, refreshing and delicious. A witty, humorous tale full of memorable, likeable characters."

—*Romantic Times*

"Unforgettable characters, believable stories, and laugh-out-loud humor. Ms. Elizabeth pens some of the best dialogue in the business."

—*A Little Romance*

## DESTINY'S EMBRACE

"Non-stop action, real-life emotion, and side-splitting humor. All the spunk and sassy wit we've come to love from the Destiny series."

—*A Little Romance*

"Ms. Elizabeth keeps readers mesmerized. . . . *Destiny's Embrace* is a wonderful frolic in time."

—*Romantic Times*

Books by Suzanne Elizabeth

*When Destiny Calls*
*Fan the Flame*
*Kiley's Storm*
*Destined to Love*
*Destiny Awaits*
*Till the End of Time*
*Destiny's Embrace*
*Destiny in Disguise*

Published by HarperPaperbacks

# Destiny
## in
# Disguise

⚔ SUZANNE ELIZABETH ⚔

**HarperPaperbacks**
*A Division of* HarperCollins*Publishers*

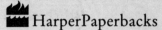 HarperPaperbacks
*A Division of* HarperCollins*Publishers*
10 East 53rd Street, New York, N.Y. 10022-5299

ISBN 0-06-108452-2

HarperCollins®, ![logo]®, HarperMonogram®, and
HarperPaperbacks™, are trademarks of HarperCollins*Publishers,* Inc.

Cover illustration by Vittorio Dangelico

First printing: June 1997

Printed in the United States of America

Visit HarperPaperbacks on the World Wide Web at
http://www.harpercollins.com/paperbacks

❖ 10 9 8 7 6 5 4 3 2 1

*For Rachel, Matthew, and Kadey Rose.
May you always know the exhilaration
and freedom of your own
self-confidence.*

*Destiny in Disguise*

**1**

**Littleville, California, 1997**

*Though it went against* everything she stood for—punctuality, responsibility, and dependability—Jane Baker packed her notebook and pens into her burlap purse and closed the Littleville library one hour early.

Despite her normally calm demeanor, Jane had been feeling restless all day, and that restlessness had nothing to do with the dry Santa Ana winds, which had been blowing ceaselessly for a week; the unnaturally hot weather; or even the gravitational pull of the moon, which was expected to be bright and full that night.

No, Jane Baker was turning thirty on this second day of June, and that fact was feeding upon her mind like a nagging headache.

Her day had started like any other: she'd awakened alone, as usual, eaten breakfast alone, as usual, and had a lovely conversation with her geranium. But for the first time being alone had really bothered her. For the first time in her life, Jane Baker felt as if she were missing out on something.

Unnerved, she'd moved headlong into her day in hopes that her odd mood would simply go away. But it hadn't. Her feelings of discontent continued, distracting her throughout the morning, disturbing her focus as she reshelved books and sifted through the library mail.

Her patience had only grown thinner and thinner as the day wore on, and when she caught a pair of teenage boys sitting in a far corner tearing the suggestive pages out of a romance novel she'd lectured them about leading productive lives before they started robbing convenience stores and ended up in prison.

The boys, of course, laughed at her on their way out the double glass doors, commenting that she was just angry because they were tampering with her one and only source of sexual fulfillment.

That remark had hit just a little too close to home.

Jane's day had only gotten worse from there. She'd barely shooed the smart-mouthed vandals outside when Paula Preston came strutting into the library and up to the checkout counter. The woman popped her chewing gum, and proceeded to go on and on about her "hot date" the night before with a visiting Hollywood casting director.

This was apparently what men liked, Jane thought as she listened politely to Paula—while trying, desperately, not to stare at Paula's tight, fire-engine-red spandex dress. Paula Preston was one of the most sought-after dates in the county; men would come from as far north as San Francisco just to eat in the diner where she worked and stare down her dusky, two-thousand-dollar-apiece cleavage as they ordered a greasy plate of bacon and eggs. It was also a well-known fact that Paula Preston had a brain roughly the size of a pea-pod. But her lack of intelligence—and generosity—didn't seem to matter to the general male populace. Paula Preston was Littleville's most valued commodity.

Jane wasn't bitter, though. Just because she'd been blessed with brains instead of a bounty of pluses in the looks department didn't mean that life wasn't worth living. It just meant that life simply wasn't fair—a lesson she'd learned years ago. She was content to spend her days sending out past-due notices and chasing necking teenagers out from behind the card catalogs. At least she *had* been content, until she'd awakened that morning with a dark cloud of doom hanging over her head.

"He's going to be casting the new Stallone movie next month," Paula told her around the large wad of bubble gum in her mouth.

Jane smiled politely, and continued stamping books with red-ink due dates. "How nice."

"Just think," Paula began, pressing both her point and her colossal breasts further into Jane's line of vision. "You might get to see *these* smashed against Sylvester Stallone's tanned chest in a movie soon."

Frankly, Jane doubted the big screen could accommodate both of them at the same time—and she didn't mean Sly and Paula.

"Don't be jealous, Plain Jane." That was the lovely nickname Jane had been gifted with as a child—by her father no less. "Someday your ship will come in. It'll be small, and rotted, and full of holes," Paula added with an evil smile, "but it'll come in."

Yes, Paula Preston was a bona fide witch, from the roots of her overly bleached hair to the tips of her red-painted toenails. But Jane was always polite. After all, she wasn't without her own little idiosyncrasies. Along with a sizable amount of intellect, Jane had been blessed with a very fertile imagination, one that could turn her into a veritable menace to society at will—all within the safe confines of her own mind, of course.

And that morning, with Paula grinning and snapping bubble gum in her face, Jane's imagination went into overdrive. She pictured herself picking up a straight-pin and popping the two oversized water balloons lolling about on her work counter with a vengeful glee that rivaled Lizzie Borden.

And it was during the midst of this imagining that Jane's conscience would normally kick in and whisper to her how wrong such an act would be. However, today Jane had heard nothing. No warning, no gentle reminder of Paula Preston's obvious cerebral inadequacies, no suggestion of what might happen to Jane herself if she followed through with such an abominable act. The only sound Jane heard in her head was the ringing of her own ears as her eyes strayed to a straight-pin lying not an arm's length away on the countertop.

Her fingers had itched with the desire to pick it up and make Paula Preston pay for every vicious thing she'd ever said to her; for all the insidious little remarks, all the mudballs slammed into the back of her head, all the times Jane had been forced to take the back way to school. . . .

"I'm here to get a book on fishing," Paula blurted out.

The interruption of her thoughts snapped Jane out of her compulsion. She blinked away the bloodthirsty image in her mind's eye and cleared her throat. "Fishing?" Despite the fact that the ocean rested not one mile from the very spot where they were standing, Jane would have laid odds that Paula Preston didn't know what a fish *was,* let alone have any *real* interest in catching one. "Why fishing?"

The blonde rolled her eyes. "Because, you dolt, the movie's about a loan shark. Duhhh."

Jane used her long, dirty-blond bangs to cover a roll of her eyes and went back to stamping books. "Top of the third shelf from the door." She would have offered Paula a Dewey decimal number, but figured that would only confuse the woman.

Jane stamped two more books, but the tanned globes of flesh barely hiding behind the scooped neckline of Paula Preston's red spandex dress didn't budge an inch from the countertop—and Jane doubted Paula would have gone anywhere without them.

Finally, Jane looked up. "Was there something else?"

Paula gave her a chilly smile, which showed off a small speck of red lipstick plastered to her front tooth. "You don't actually expect me to get the book myself, do you? Isn't that *your* pathetic little job?"

Jane's chest tightened. This was the exact sort of abuse she'd put up with since childhood. Her nemesis might be dumb and pumped full of silicon, but Jane Baker had feared Paula Preston since the age of six when Paula had tripped her in the school parking lot before kindergarten, stolen her plaid skirt, and left her to face the world wearing nothing but a little cotton shirt and pair of worn, Wonder Woman panties. For some reason Jane had always brought out the worst in Paula Preston.

Jane closed her ink pad and carefully set her stamper down sideways on the metal lid. She slipped off the stool, hating the *thrwaaap* sound that resulted from her sweaty thighs skidding across vinyl, and hating Paula's responding snicker even more. She walked across the polished gray and silver linoleum floor toward the third bookshelf from the front doors, and used a small metal stepladder to find the book she felt Paula was after. *As if the woman can even read,* she grumbled to herself.

Her eyes lit on *Big Game Fishing in the Pacific.* She pulled out the thin book, climbed down the stepladder, and headed back to her work counter.

Maybe if Jane hadn't felt so intimidated in that moment she might have noticed the wicked little gleam in Paula Preston's big blue eyes.

She sat back down on her stool, and something went *squish* beneath her.

She leaped back up and heard the metal clank of something hitting the floor at her feet. It was her red ink pad.

Gasping, she pulled her best white cotton skirt around to the front and stared in desperation at the bright red stain on the back panel. A stain that wouldn't come out with all the Clorox in the world.

"Looks like your mattress gave out, Janey," Paula remarked, grinning from pert little ear to pert little ear. "You should have definitely gone for a heavy-flow pad today."

Jane stared at her for a long moment, her expression giving away none of the fury she was feeling on the inside. She wanted to scream but held in her rage and felt tears burn her eyes instead. She wasn't about to give Paula the satisfaction of seeing her cry, though, so she held that impulse in as well.

Quietly, calmly, she picked up her ink pad and set it back on the counter. She stamped Paula's fishing book, all the while holding back a flood of tears, and couldn't find the courage to so much as even look up as Paula Preston turned and sauntered out of the library.

Jane dropped her face into her hands and mentally castigated herself for not uttering a single word in her own defense. She'd been taunted and teased all her life, and never, not once, had she ever stood up for herself. Turn the other cheek, that's what her mother had always told her to do, and that's exactly what Jane had always done. Although she suspected, as did everyone else in town, that her cheek-turning was done more out of fear than any sense of Christian charity. Just about everything Jane Baker did or didn't do tended to be motivated by fear.

For thirty years her entire existence had been a series of embarrassments and catastrophes, and she had absolutely nothing to show for herself but a "pathetic little job" and an empty little life.

And that's why Jane had decided to close the library one full hour early, at 3:00 instead of 4:00.

It was quite an act of defiance for Jane. But if Mr. Cleery, the library's curator, got upset with her, she'd simply tell him that she hadn't been feeling well. And that wasn't exactly a lie.

She would go home and celebrate her thirtieth birthday by curling up in front of her television set, eating her way through an entire box of bonbons, and drinking her way through a case of root beer. Surely by tomorrow she'd be feeling better . . . and then she could get back to muddling through her insignificant life.

It was another bright, joyous day in heaven, with cherubs singing heralds to each man rejoining the spirit world, with sweet, mellow trumpets sounding off jubilantly each time a new soul found its place on earth, and with angels and saints alike working side by side to make life on the blue planet below just a little easier than it might have otherwise been.

However, things being on earth as they are in heaven, not everything always went as planned in paradise. Such was the case in the Department of Spiritual Affairs this second day of June at a quarter to five standard earth time. Stella, the assistant to the director, was sitting at her Henry VIII desk with her brown leather chair tipped back far enough to lift her range of vision. She was quite a bit smaller than the average angel, with short dark hair, tiny eyes, and even tinier features.

She drew a deep breath, narrowed her dark eyes, and leveled them on the angel standing before her. He was the newest member of her department, having previously been assigned to the Disputer's office, and she'd regretted his transfer from the first moment of his induction: he'd spent more time being reprimanded in her office than Moses had spent in the desert.

"Nelson," she stated coolly, barely keeping her normally placid temper in check. "I find myself at a loss about what to do with you."

"I should think that would be obvious, madam," he responded insolently. "My talents lie in disputing, not in playing shepherd to hapless earthbounds whose only goal in life is to find the perfect light beer to go with a cheeseburger."

"Mrs. Stephens has filed a formal complaint."

Nelson gasped. "How was *I* to know the woman was depressed?" he replied impatiently. "I was simply trying to help her—"

"And you did help her." Stella folded her arms and

flashed him a cutting smile. "Right out a third-story window."

"I did *apologize* to the woman." And upon hearing that it was his fault that she'd died before originally planned, Mrs. Elmira Stephens had hauled off and clobbered him with her newly acquired halo.

"An apology can hardly make up for the forty or so years of spiritual growth she's missed out on because of your neglect, Nelson. You cut the woman's life in half, for heaven's sake."

Nelson pursed his lips to keep from arguing the point any further. He really had only been trying to help Mrs. Stephens when he'd suggested to her that the light green gown she'd chosen to wear to the charity benefit that night made her look like a giant lime. He hadn't been aware at the time that her husband had just announced he was leaving her for a younger woman, that her employer had only that afternoon suggested an early retirement because of the increasing arthritis in her hands, and that her yearly physical that morning had revealed the beginnings of menopause.

Stella would argue that as her spiritual guide he was supposed to have known these things. But, feeling that the woman could certainly hold her own for a while, Nelson had occupied himself with other things that day and hadn't paid either of his two clients much attention. Thus, when he'd finally turned on the large screen on the wall behind his desk and seen what Mrs. Stephens had chosen to wear that night, his reaction had been instinctive instead of based on any kind of qualified knowledge.

*You look like a missing member of a fruit bowl,* he'd commented to her malleable mind. *Carry a lemon in your hand and you can go as a giant bottle of soda.*

Imagine his surprise when the woman had taken one look at herself in the mirror, burst into tears, and done a swan dive out her apartment window.

Under the steady, pinpointed heat of Stella's glare, Nelson took a deep breath and tugged on the lapels of his pristine white Armani jacket. All right, he *was* feeling a bit ashamed—which accounted for his piqued and somewhat defensive posture—but it was high time that this foolishness ended and he was returned to the department where he rightfully belonged: Disputing. Guardianship just wasn't his forte. Yes, at times he did feel vaguely aggrieved for those hapless souls on earth. The answers to life's little dilemmas were so painfully clear, so simple in their essence, but those below were either too ignorant, too distracted, or too uncaring to notice.

As an angel with normally very little patience, Nelson's frustration with his new job was practically tangible. And, though contrite over Mrs. Stephens's regrettable tragedy, he could only hope that it would prove, once and for all, that he was not cut out to be a spiritual guide.

Stella's harsh glare lasted another moment before she finally looked away and heaved a heavy sigh of resignation. "I cannot, in all good conscience, transfer you back." Nelson's pale face reddened to a deep, hot shade of red that climbed clear to the roots of his white-blond hair. The deep cleft in his prominent chin quivered as he struggled to restrain himself. "How can you," he sputtered, "in all good conscience, allow me to *continue*?"

"You were placed here in my department for a reason, in hopes that direct contact with earthly souls would temper your predispositions and general lack of patience toward them. As a disputer you are very accomplished, Nelson, however you lack the compassion required to remain unbiased. Until such time that you begin to show compassion and understanding, this department is where you shall remain."

Resenting her businesslike manner in the face of his defeat, Nelson pulled back his shoulders and straightened to his full height, which, in comparison to Stella's, was a considerable distance up, and which also explained why she was forced to tip her chair back even further to keep his face in her range of vision. "I want it on record that I heartily disagree with this decision," he blustered.

"So noted. Now. As for your remaining client, Miss Baker—"

"She is timid, self-deprecating, and socially underdeveloped," he cut in. "And here I thought you weren't going to be assigning me a hamster," he added with a wry twist of his thin lips.

"Which is why anyone would have to be deliberately inept to throw a kink into her quiet, orderly life. Simply keep an eye on her, Nelson, throw a little whisper of self-confidence her way every now and again, and you *should* do just fine."

So this is what his illustrious career had come to? Playing nursemaid to Jane Baker. A woman so pointless that she didn't even have a mission in life.

Every single soul sent down to earth had a mission, small or large, momentous or inconsequential. It was the token agreed upon for the opportunity to grow spiritually by attaining mortal flesh. But, as in a few rare occasions, a mistake had occurred during Jane Baker's birth and she had been sent to the wrong place in time. Once old enough to deal with the shock, misplaced souls were generally relocated to their rightful time frames and all was set right with the world. However, because of her experiences growing up in the twentieth century, Jane Baker had been deemed incapable of surviving in the nineteenth century, the time where she rightfully belonged. It had been decided that she would be better off remaining exactly where she was.

Thus Jane Baker would never know her true potential, never feel the joy of reconnecting with her spiritual friends and family, and never experience the exhilaration of merging with her soul mate.

At times Nelson actually felt sorry for the woman.

Stella folded her small hands in her lap. "As we've discussed before, your main course with Miss Baker is to bring her out of her shell so that she will at least be capable of enjoying the life she has for the time she has left."

"And may I ask how much time that will be?" Dare he hope that the nonessential Miss Baker only had months—weeks—until she rejoined the spirit world?

"Forty-three years."

Nelson slumped forward.

"Need I remind you of the consequences if you fail again, Nelson?"

"No, you need not." He'd just spent two days standing at the gates of heaven signing in new arrivals from the Hell's Angels' quadrant. The *adventure* was permanently engraved in his brain.

"Another mishap like the last, and you will find yourself spending a full week registering incoming from the Viking era."

Nelson let out a sharp gasp. "You *wouldn't*?"

Stella smiled, obviously relishing the image. "Keep a

close eye on Miss Baker, Nelson. And in forty-three years we'll see about moving you up to something a little more challenging, say. . . a happily married mother of three?"

Nelson straightened. As far as he was concerned, he would have no other clients. He would prove himself once and for all with Miss Baker, and then respectfully request a transfer out of this frivolous department and back to a disputer's desk where his talents were of value. "I assure you, madam," he said confidently, "my client will be given the tenderest of attentions."

"Yes, well, thankfully Miss Baker lives in a one-story house," Stella responded dryly. "So I suppose the worst we can anticipate is a nasty twist of an ankle."

# 2

*Jane stood at the top* of the cement steps out-side the library, staring out over Littleville's city square. She'd turned her white skirt backward so that the large, red ink stain was in the front, resting against her left thigh—still unsightly, but no longer an embarrassing calamity.

As if she had anyone to impress. The last time a man had even looked sideways at her, she'd tripped over a crack in the sidewalk and fallen flat on her face.

She glanced down at her feet and wiggled her toes in her flat-heeled, sensible shoes. Sensible, dependable Jane. As plain and timid as a field mouse.

A thirty-year-old field mouse.

As she walked down the steps and through the open courtyard, she felt every second of those thirty years weighing her down like an anchor. Pulling her farther and farther into the cold, murky darkness of despair.

The hot desert wind danced across her face and toyed with her ponytail of unremarkable dark blond as she began her short walk home. Her destiny, it seemed, had been decided at birth—one useless, solitary life coming right up. Only women like Paula Preston lived excitement and dated Hollywood casting directors. Jane snorted ironically; the funny thing was, she actually admired Paula in an odd sort of way. Paula Preston had courage. The kind Jane could only dream of. How she wished she could bulldoze through life the way Paula Preston did without any thought to what the rest of the world might be thinking.

But Jane did worry about what the rest of the world thought. She even worried about what the dead world thought. Her mother had been gone for almost a year now, and she still felt as if the woman were watching her every move and shaking her head with disapproval.

Which brought up another point: Jane supposed the stress from her mother's lingering battle with cancer could have finally caught up with her—Dr. Stuart had warned her about that possibility. Jane hadn't believed him at the funeral, because at the time she hadn't felt a thing but an overwhelming sense of relief that it was finally over. She'd put off college to stay home with her widowed mother and see her through the *rough spots*. After ten long years of rough spots, Jane had been very anxious to get started with her life.

But it had been almost a year since Mary Baker's death, and Jane had yet to request a single application form from any of the local colleges. It was becoming apparent to her, and half the town, that her mother's illness had only been yet another excuse for her to run from life. She'd never been all that comfortable with the idea of leaving home in the first place.

Jane tried to comfort herself with the possibility that maybe she'd simply outgrown her need for college.

Maybe she felt more comfortable in familiar surroundings? Maybe she was perfectly satisfied with the life she had?

But deep down inside she knew that wasn't true.

She rounded the corner onto Maple and stopped in front of her house. Her mother's house. Although Jane made plenty of money, she'd been too intimidated by the thought of a mortgage to sell the drafty old home where she'd grown up and move to a newer, better neighborhood. Besides, this house was only three blocks away from the library. Any farther and she'd have to buy a car and drive—something else that intimidated her.

Oh sure, she could take a driving class and practice on quiet, safe roads, but that would interrupt her regimented routine. And her routine was the only thing that gave her any peace. Six days out of the week she opened the library doors precisely at eight, and closed them precisely at four. On Sundays she attended church, via the city bus, and took books to the local retirement home. And every evening she settled in front of the television for dinner for one.

She'd never had a boyfriend, never even had a date for that matter—unless you counted Freddy Pendergraff, who'd only asked her to the sixth grade dance on a dare. As a matter of fact, she'd long ago given up hoping her Prince Charming would come along and sweep her off her feet; her mother had always told her "happily ever after" was silly nonsense anyway.

In short, Jane lived in a staid, comfortable rut, and intended to keep things that way. Change was just too frightening a concept to even consider. After all, what if the changes she made were wrong and put her in an even worse predicament than she was already in?

She stared up at her empty front porch, where there were no extra pairs of shoes to signify other residents. No dog barked a greeting to her from the wide front window. No toys were left carelessly in the driveway. The house looked vacant, and no one and nothing waited for her inside except Felix, her very quiet and very safe geranium.

She slowly climbed the five narrow cement steps and headed down the long walkway toward her front door. Each echoing *clop* of her shoes pounded out the predictable rhythm that had been her thirty-year life, and suddenly she wasn't sure she wanted to stumble through another thirty. Certainly no one would miss her—or even care—if she mixed an entire bottle of sleeping pills in with her birthday mashed potatoes. She'd sit in her easy chair with the glow of prime time reflecting on her face and slowly drift off to sleep. Forever. How easy. How comforting. How . . .

Jane stopped suddenly. For the sake of her sanity, she couldn't take another step—not one more forward motion in the direction she'd been heading all her life. She was actually contemplating killing herself. In all that had happened to her—or hadn't happened to her—in her thirty years, she'd never once considered ending her life. And the truly frightening thing was . . . the idea was very inviting. She looked up at the thick maple tree in her front yard, the one she used to climb when she was little, and then at the blue sky above her head where veils of white clouds were drifting by in the hot breeze. There had to be more to life than what she already knew. More than just the small space of air surrounding her. There was supposedly an entire world out there, one reputed to hold unlimited possibilities. But where were *her* possibilities? Where were *her* chances? They never seemed to come her way. And now, here she stood, considering ending her chances once and for all.

She couldn't believe it. She wouldn't do it! If those opportunities and chances wouldn't come to her, then she simply had to find the courage to go out and get them!

She glanced around her yard. Compared to the others in the neighborhood it looked plain and dull. Reflective of her life. She could buy some seeds this weekend and plant some flowers. The expansive bed beneath the front window was empty. It could use a shrub or two. She took a step toward the bed, but stopped just short of placing her foot on the grass. How long had it been since she'd walked on her grass except to mow it? Like a miserly old woman, she'd always used the front walk.

Well, that was about to change.

Setting her chin, she turned and marched right back down the walkway, and back down the five narrow cement steps to the sidewalk. She gave the five-foot rock wall supporting her front yard an assessing look. She'd climbed it repeatedly as a child. She could certainly do the same now. Practically buzzing with excitement and anxiety, she stepped forward and set her foot on the edge of a jagged rock. Then she slowly began to pull herself up the retaining wall by her fingertips. She found a sturdy place for her other foot, and pulled herself up even higher. Fear nagged at her like an overprotective friend, but Jane shoved the feeling aside and continued up the wall.

"Jane Baker?" old Mrs. Hatterly called from the porch of the small house across the street. "What the dickens are you doin'?"

"I'm living, Mrs. Hatterly!" Jane called back, struggling with her next foothold—this wasn't as easy as she remembered. "I'm . . . I'm really living!"

"You're gonna break your neck, is what you're gonna do!" the old woman screeched back.

"Nonsense, Mrs. Hatterly," Jane replied, out of breath. She gained a foothold on another rock and pulled herself up even higher. "Life is meant to be lived!"

Jane was now eye level with her lawn, and adrenaline was pumping through her body like a raging fire, making her heart pound and her hands shake. Finally, she reached the top, heaved herself up, and straightened to a standing position on the wide, uneven ledge. "See, Mrs. Hatterly," she called, feeling her first burst of pride in years. "It's just a teeny little rock wa . . . waaaa—waahh-hhhh!"

Her center of gravity suddenly shifted backward. She flailed her arms around her head like the twin rotors on a helicopter as she frantically tried to balance herself. She shifted one foot, then the other, but in the flash of a moment Jane Baker's entire inconsequential life flashed before her eyes. She let out a piercing scream. And toppled backward to the cement sidewalk below.

More than anything else in the world, Nelson loved a good game of solitaire. In fact at times he could get so caught up in one that the rest of the world simply ceased to exist. After his rather tense meeting with his superior, he'd decided to indulge himself with a round or two.

Miss Jane Baker was coming right along—he'd

checked in on her only the night before. Nothing new or troubling was happening to her, which was little surprise considering her life was about as interesting as a shadow creeping across a paved road. Certainly the woman could handle shuffling back and forth to work and stamping a few books all on her own for a day.

All in all, Jane Baker was relatively low-maintenance. Nelson did nothing but remind her of morals she already knew, point out facts she'd long before come to understand, and recommend things that had usually already occurred to her.

Nelson smiled and laid down his final king. "Looks like I win again." In fact, with only one client to claim his attention now, it looked as if his luck might finally be changing for the better.

The buzzer on his intercom sounded, rattling against his desktop. He scowled at the interruption and hit the button with his palm. "Yes? What is it?"

"Your client is here to see you, sir," the receptionist replied.

Nelson frowned. "My client?"

"Yes, sir. Your client. Miss Baker."

The breath shot out of Nelson's lungs so fast that if he weren't already dead he would have thought he was having another coronary. He whipped around in his chair and hit the button that turned on his viewing screen. The large wall monitor came to life with nothing but hissing static—just as it had with Mrs. Elmira Stephens after she'd done a half-gainer out her third-floor window.

"Oh dear *God!*" Nelson cried, lunging up from his chair. "She's *dead*? The woman is *dead?!* I leave her for twelve *teeny* little hours and she goes off and gets herself *killed!*"

And then he remembered what Stella had said—more to the point, what she'd threatened—and visions of hulking, smelly Vikings began dancing through his mind, raising the hair on his arms and bulging his blue eyes.

The buzzer on his desk rattled again. "Sir, your client is waiting," the receptionist reminded.

Nelson did a little dance of uncertainty and then finally managed to bring himself under control. "Okay," he said to himself. He took a deep, cleansing breath. "Like all incoming, the woman is confused, frightened, a *bit* groggy. . . .What to do . . . what to do . . . "

He tapped his long fingers on his desk and tried to think the situation through.

"I've got it," he finally said. "I've got it. I'll just send her right back where she came from. It's done all the time," he said with a nervous laugh. "Mistakes are made. Mistakes are rectified. It's back to your body you go, Miss Baker. And no one need *ever* be the wiser."

He straightened, adjusted his white tie and lapels, and plastered a warm, welcoming smile on his face. Then he strode forward and opened his door to the waiting room beyond.

He knew her right away among the ten or so others waiting to see their spiritual guides. As usual, a lively conversation was occurring upon the sofas. The incoming were trading knowledge, trying to understand what had happened to them. But Jane Baker was hunched on the white couch with her head tucked down between her shoulders like a giant turtle facing mortal danger. She looked as if she wished the entire couch would swallow her whole.

And Nelson was wishing the exact same thing.

"Miss Baker?" he called to her. Her head popped up and she stared at him with wide green eyes. "Won't you come in?" he said, forcing his smile broader.

She stood slowly, with her arms clutched tightly around herself, and began walking toward him. He fought the impulse to shout at her to hurry, that they didn't have much time if they were to go about all this without being found out, but he bit his tongue and waited patiently as she edged past him and into his office.

"Where am I?" she whispered as he closed his door.

"Have a seat, Miss Baker."

She lowered herself into the padded white chair across from his desk and stared bleakly up at him. "Did I . . . did I do something wrong?"

*Yes!* he wanted to snap back. *You went and died on me!* But he continued to force a smile, and said instead, "Miss Baker, to put it quite bluntly . . . you're dead."

If it were possible, her eyes grew even rounder. They turned an intense shade of emerald green as she leaned toward him. "I beg your pardon?"

Nelson punched a few buttons and called up her data on his desk terminal. The date and method of her death popped up on the wall monitor behind him. "You"—he gritted his teeth as he read what had happened. "You *fell* from the retaining wall surrounding your lawn? What in *great* tarnation were you doing scaling a *five-foot* rock wall?" he demanded.

Jane Baker flinched, and burrowed back into her chair. "I . . . I was . . . trying something new, and—"

"*Something new*? Well how about *death,* Miss Baker? Is that *new enough* for ya?"

Tears beaded on her lashes. "Actually that was what I was trying to avoid."

Her tears tugged at him. "Oh, for heaven's sake. Don't start weeping." He handed her the silk kerchief from the breast pocket of his suit.

"But . . . but you just said I was dead," she replied through an avalanche of tears.

"Yes, however"—he cringed as she blew her nose into his kerchief—"I believe I can rectify the situation."

"Rectify?"

She held the handkerchief out to him. He accepted it with two fingers and promptly tossed it into the wastebasket. "I intend to send you back to your body," he explained in simple terms.

"You can do that?"

"Of course." At least he believed he could. "Sending you back is a *very* simple process. And then you'll have a lovely near-death experience to share with all your friends. Won't that be nice?"

"Yes, I . . . I suppose so."

"Good. Now . . ." He turned to his desk terminal, and typed in Jane Baker's full name and the time and place where her body was located. A menu popped up prompting him to indicate where he would like to send her. Nelson smirked at how easy the process was, and scoffed inwardly at how complicated Stella had made temporal relocations out to be. He highlighted RESTORE CORRECT TEMPORAL SIGHT, and hit enter. The terminal started churning softly and he turned and smiled at his client. "There," he said. "All better."

He crossed the room and opened his office door. "The receptionist will take things from here. Back to life with you, Miss Baker."

"I only wanted to try something different," she said, meek and bleary-eyed, as she passed him on her way back into the waiting room. "It was just a tiny little rock wall. . . ."

Nelson continued to smile tightly as he shut his door. Then he dropped all pretense, crossed to his desk, and dropped down into his chair where he heaved a great sigh of relief. "Oh, and in the future, Miss Baker," he said to the empty room, *"try to avoid killing yourself!"*

# 3

*It was the most exquisite feeling:* total peace, complete joy, absolute fulfillment.

Jane was drifting, floating through the brightest, warmest light. A light that flowed in and out of her, wrapped around her, became part of her, and filled her with love and hope. For the first time in her life, she felt no fear.

And then the light began to fade.

Jane clung to the sensations with all her might, but as the light continued to wane so did its effects. Its infusing warmth began to vanish, leaving her cold, confused, and, once again, afraid. . . .

When Jane's soul finally settled back into her body, a jarring chill shook through her like a bolt of electricity. She pulled a sharp, sudden breath into her lungs that caused her skin to prickle and her lips to tingle. She tried to focus, but found her mind sluggish and her thoughts muddy. Her head hurt. It felt as if it had been split in two and put back together wrong, and she let out a deep groan.

Finally memories of that afternoon gradually began to come back to her: her birthday, Paula, her fiasco with the rock wall. No wonder her head hurt so much; she was lucky she hadn't broken her neck.

The hot sun beat down on her from above, glaring through her eyelids, and making her clothes warm against her skin. She wanted to sit up, but her limbs felt weighted, impossibly heavy, and she couldn't quite find the strength to open her eyes just yet. Good lord, she hoped she wasn't paralyzed. What an irony that would be. Poor Jane Baker. She'd never had the courage to try anything new. And then one day she'd gotten a wild hair, climbed a rock wall, and rendered herself incapable of ever trying anything new again.

Focusing all her mental energies, Jane finally managed to twitch her big toe. A wave of relief swept through her, and she scoffed at what the blond man had said, that she was dead. How preposterous—

*Blond man?*

Her train of thought came to a sudden grinding halt.

And then the realization dawned on her: she had odd, fragmented memories of a tall, blond man in an all-white suit telling her she was dead. In fact, the cold, sarcastic edge to his voice still rang clearly through her mind: *You fell from the retaining wall surrounding your lawn?*

She could still envision the dimple in his chin quivering as he forced a polite smile, and could see his jaw work as he clenched his teeth to hold back his irritation with her.

She'd never had such a tangible dream before, but then it wasn't every day that she cracked her head on the cement and lost consciousness. She was lucky to be alive.

She finally gave a mental shrug and disregarded the dream entirely, chalking it up to trauma to the brain and too many reruns of "Highway to Heaven"—

"Get up."

Jane grimaced at the gruff, unfamiliar voice. She'd finally managed to slowly lift one hand, and was massaging her aching forehead. Apparently she was blocking someone's path on the sidewalk. "Could you . . . could you please just give me a moment?"

Without further warning, she was taken by the front of her shirt and wrenched to her feet. "I don't intend to waste one more second on you, lady."

Stunned, Jane cracked open her eyes and struggled to bring into focus the man who had a large leather-gloved hand clamped to the front of her shirt. "I . . . I beg your—"

"Oh, don't bother to beg. That would only embarrass us both. You know, I should shoot you where you stand for leading me on this wild-goose chase. You're lucky I'm in such a good mood."

Still dazed, and not having the slightest idea what the man was going on about, Jane attempted to take a step back from him. But he yanked her closer.

Her nose came flat against his hard, wide chest covered in blue-striped cotton, her nostrils flared with his scent of sun and musky male sweat, and she swallowed hard at the taut lump of apprehension that lodged tightly in her throat.

She lifted her gaze higher, past his broad shoulders, up his corded, tanned neck, and to his darkly stubbled chin. His lips were full and broad, his nose long and narrow, and he was glaring down at her with a pair of steel-blue eyes hooded in heavy, black eyebrows. His dark hair was curling carelessly over his ears, and hanging over his forehead. His jaw was set, his eyes were sharp, and he was either smirking at her sardonically, or sneering at her maniacally. Either way, he was the roughest looking man Jane had ever seen.

"Who . . . ? Who are you?" she asked tremulously.

"Your biggest nightmare," he replied darkly. Jane's eyes rounded, and instinct took over: she threw back her head and let out a scream shrill enough to pierce an eardrum.

The man swore beneath his breath and quickly cut her off by clamping his free hand over her mouth. Their gazes locked, his sharp and unpredictable, hers wide and terrified, and her knees went weak—if he hadn't still been holding her by the front of her shirt, she would have crumpled to the ground at his feet.

Jane struggled to focus, to keep fear from overwhelming her. But she couldn't think beyond the danger staring her in the face, couldn't move past the tight grip of terror squeezing her heart; she could barely even breathe.

"Screaming isn't going to do you one damn bit of good, lady," her attacker stated into her face. "So save your goddamn breath—and my goddamn ears."

Sure she was about to die a horrible, violent death, Jane felt tears burn into her eyes. She thought of Mrs. Hatterly living alone and defenseless across the street. Poor old Mrs. Hatterly. The frail woman would be helpless against this brutal predator who apparently attacked women at their weakest moments. *Run, Mrs. Hatterly!* Jane cried out mentally. *Run and lock your doors!*

Oh, why couldn't she have just stuck with her quiet

little staid life and left well enough alone? What in the *world* had she been thinking?

"I'm gonna give you one chance." He moved his tanned face closer to hers, until she could see the fine lines around his steel-blue eyes. "You give me a single ounce of trouble, and I'm gonna tie you up."

Instead of snapping her neck, which she half expected him to do at any moment, he removed his hand from her mouth and released his tight grip on her shirt. Jane finally allowed herself to breathe again, and then he held a rigid finger up in front of her nose. "Not one ounce of trouble," he reiterated.

She nodded, although the action was more like a stiff jerk, and was vastly relieved when he finally stepped back from her—vastly relieved, that is, until she got a good look at what he was wearing strapped to his right hip: a pearl-handled pistol, sheathed in a thick, black-leather holster. She swallowed down a gasp, and returned her attention to his face, where she found him staring at her intently. His gaze swept her over from head to toe, and then a scowl shadowed his features as his examination stopped at her skirt. "Did you hurt yourself?"

Jane glanced down at the large red stain so prominent on her white cotton skirt. "N-no. It's . . . it's just ink."

He nodded. "Good. Lift it."

She blinked. Surely she'd misunderstood him. "Wh-what?"

He crossed his arms over his broad chest. "You heard me. Lift the skirt."

Jane's throat went into a spasm. "B-but—"

Apparently not interested in arguing the point any further, he marched forward, grabbed the hem of her calf-length skirt, and wrenched it up over her head. Jane let out a strangled cry as her face was suddenly covered by heavy white cotton and the warm heat of the afternoon sun settled over her bare thighs. She could only stand there shaking, too afraid to move. But before her fertile mind could conjure up any of the numerous dastardly deeds this man might consider doing to her, he threw her skirt back down over her exposed underwear.

"P-please don't . . . don't hurt me." She was breathing hard, and had her arms crossed protectively over her chest.

He smiled crookedly at her, which was almost as terrifying to her as his icy glare. "I wouldn't dream of it. Now mount up."

She swallowed in hesitation and confusion. "M-mount up?"

"I brought your horse with me."

"My horse?" For the first time since opening her eyes, Jane allowed herself to look at something besides her attacker and her jaw dropped open in shock. She was standing in a grassy meadow filled with orange and yellow wildflowers. Five feet away from her a wide river was drifting lazily over slick, mossy rocks. She was utterly surrounded on all sides by a fortress of thick, towering trees. And directly in front of her a sheer rock cliff shot majestically over one hundred feet into the blue, blue sky above.

She wasn't in Littleville anymore.

By the time Jane's terrified gaze reconnected with that of her attacker, another ear-piercing scream was building in her chest. He gave her a warning look, one that was, unfortunately, completely lost on her in the heat of panic. She opened her mouth and the scream tore from her throat, echoing off the river and the rocky cliff, sending birds scattering from the surrounding trees. The frightening man lunged for her—which only made Jane scream louder—and once again clamped his hand over her mouth.

"This little fit of yours isn't going to work, lady!" he shouted above her muffled wail. "Not any more than everything else you've tried so far!"

To the best of Jane's knowledge all she'd *tried so far* was terror, panic, and complete submission. Perhaps a little applied force might work to her advantage.

She bit down on his hand with all her might. And got nothing but a mouthful of dirty leather.

She looked warily up into his face, and found his expression as calm as it had been before. "Bite me again," he said slowly, "and you'll get bit back."

Jane nodded, hoping her ready acquiescence would make him step back from her again. He was threatening enough standing a few feet away; having him this close, his tall, broad body towering above her own, was practically debilitating.

"Now. Are you all screamed out yet?"

She nodded again.

"Good." He pulled his hand away from her mouth. "Then let's try this again." He gestured in the direction behind her. "Your horse."

Jane turned slowly, only to find the largest equine animal she'd ever seen chewing on grass and flowers behind her. It was sleek, dark brown, and roughly the size of a small minivan. And she wasn't about to get within twenty feet of it. A fact she emphasized by backing up a few paces.

She backed right up against the man standing,

steadfastly, behind her. "Is there a problem?" he said softly into her ear.

She felt a tingle of heat on the side of her neck—his breath as it slid over her skin—and her heart give a lurch in response. She turned quickly, moving away from him in astonishment, but her fear quickly renewed itself when she got a good look at his intense, determined face once again.

"Did you and your horse have a little tiff?" he asked dryly.

"That isn't . . . my horse," she managed to croak. He gave the animal a quizzical look, one that was dramatic, to say the least.

"Really? Then why are all your belongings stuffed into the saddlebags?"

Jane gave the horse and its saddlebags a surprised glance, and then turned dumbfounded eyes on her kidnapper. "I have . . . no idea."

He released a drawn-out sigh. "Look, lady. No more trouble, remember? I'm too damn tired for this shit."

Right. No more trouble. Or who knew what might happen to her? She could be found floating face first in that treacherous river over there. Staked out beneath the hot sun on an anthill. Carved into little pieces and buried beneath the various rocks and trees surrounding her. Good God, what had happened to her? How in the world had she fallen into this dark demon's hands? What kind of man kidnapped a woman while she was lying unconscious on a sidewalk?

She would be wise to do what he said. However, there was one small problem. She had no idea how to ride a horse. "I—" She swallowed at the dryness still clinging to her throat. "I don't know how to . . . to—"

He folded his arms over his chest again, making himself look like a one-man wall. "To what? Go along peacefully? Do as you're told? Keep your mouth shut?"

Actually, Jane was pretty good at doing all of the above. Which led her to her next question. "Why are you doing this to me?" she asked, hoping her weak voice hadn't sounded as pathetic to his ears as it had to hers.

"I guess I'm just bored," he replied sarcastically.

"W-well, there . . . there must be something I can do to . . . to convince you to let me go."

He cocked his head at her, and the bright sunlight glinted blue streaks in his dark hair. He studied her for a long moment, his glittering gaze traveling slowly across her face and lingering over her body. The intense perusal sent a flood of warmth snaking through Jane's insides, and she quickly looked down at her feet to hide her discomfort. "'Preciate the offer, ma'am," he finally drawled. "Maybe I'll take ya up on it later."

Realizing his implication, all the color drained from Jane's face. "*That* was certainly *not* what I meant," she stated boldly and without thinking.

"Then what exactly did you mean?" he asked pointedly. "That you might cook me a nice dinner and I'd forget this whole thing? That maybe I'd settle for a few trinkets and your undying gratitude in exchange for letting you ride out of here with no questions asked? Or were you simply hoping I'd get a fit of conscience and let you go for nothing in return?"

Jane wasn't at all sure what she'd meant to offer him in exchange for her freedom. But sex had been the farthest thing from her mind—in fact, she was a bit stunned that it hadn't been the farthest thing from his.

"Look, enough with the games. After the week I've

had, I deserve some peace." He turned to the white horse grazing behind him, and began tightening the saddle cinch. "You've got till the count of five to get up on that horse before I put you on it myself."

He seemed so casual, so nonthreatening with his back to her, that Jane actually decided to push her luck just one more time. "Look, I-I'm feeling a little confused. If you could just tell me what happened after I fell off the wall—"

He turned toward her so fast that Jane stumbled backward and tripped over her own feet. She fell into the tall grass and flowers, making the horse grazing behind her snort in surprise. She scooted backward, trying to get away as her powerful, dark abductor stalked toward her.

"Save the terrified victim act," he stated, taking her by the arm and hauling her to her feet again. "You may be good at conning most men out of just about anything, but your pretty little smile and your wide green eyes are not gonna change my mind about taking you in."

Well, now she *knew* he was insane. Pretty little smile? Her smile was about as pretty as his horse's. And as for his other accusation, she couldn't manipulate a man into paying his overdue library charges, let alone "con him out of just about anything."

"Take me in where?" she dared to ask.

He smiled coldly. "Lady, you're about to finally experience the inside of an eight-by-ten cell."

Jane's mind raced in so many different directions that she was rendered completely incapable of responding.

"You'll be jailed, tried for murder"—he shrugged— "and most likely hanged. Probably all in the same day."

Hanged! Jane wouldn't have thought it possible, but

the man had managed to terrify her even more, and panic finally overtook her instincts for survival. "I don't know what you're talking about!" she shouted. "Why are you doing this to me? Why—"

She continued to shout frantically as he took her beneath the arms and hoisted her up into the air like a rag doll. But, instead of throwing her in the river, which she half-expected him to do, he carried her to her supposed horse and dropped her down sideways into the saddle. Jane stopped shouting and focused her energies on clinging to the saddle horn to steady herself.

"Ready?" her abductor said, smiling cheerfully up at her.

Jane stared at him in terror. She was certainly poised and ready to break her neck!

He took up her horse's reins, but then paused to look back at her one final time. "By the way. Try getting away . . . and I'll take advantage of that dead-or-alive clause and shoot you myself."

With that horrifying threat planted firmly in Jane's mind, she held on tightly as her horse was led in a lumbering, rocking gait to the white horse grazing nearby. Her kidnapper took up a black felt cowboy hat that was propped on his saddle horn and pulled it down onto his head. Then he flashed her one last bright smile and swung up into his saddle with all the grace of someone who'd done it a thousand times before. He clicked to his horse, and headed off down a narrow, worn trail through the foliage with her in tow.

Tears welled in Jane's eyes. She'd been kidnapped by a maniac—a *homicidal* maniac, and she had no idea why. She knew she needed to get away from him, but she was too terrified of what might happen if she tried to escape and failed.

It seemed the only thing she could do was stay calm and do exactly as she was told. Certainly someone had seen him carrying her away from where she'd fallen on the sidewalk—Mrs. Hatterly at least. The police would be looking for her. She simply had to stay alive long enough to be rescued.

The woman was lucky to be alive.

Though risky, it had been a work of pure genius when she'd sent her horse off without her. Dolan had tracked the damn animal for half a day before catching up to it, and by then she'd had a five-hour head start in the opposite direction. He'd figured her to be halfway to Mexico by then.

But, like magic, not two hours later Dolan had come across her lying in a field. His first thought was that she was dead, killed by animals or renegades. But as he got closer to her, he'd realized she was fast asleep. The woman had felt so confident in her plan to escape him, and, apparently, so certain of his stupidity, that she'd taken the time to steal herself a nap.

He'd just about taken her by the throat instead of the front of her shirt. She'd not only made him *feel* like a goddamn fool for the past week, she'd made him *look* like one. For seven long, frustrating days and nights he'd tracked her, but she'd always managed to stay one step ahead of him. She was as slippery as a rattlesnake, and twice as unpredictable.

Dolan could honestly say that he'd never had such a difficult time hunting down a bounty. But now that he had his hands on the lovely lady outlaw he wasn't about to let her get away, no matter how bemused and befuddled she acted—an obvious tactic to win him over.

Hell, it should have been clear to her by now, after playing cat and mouse with him for the past week, that her tactics weren't going to work on him, that this was one instance where the charming and tenacious Miss Rose Diamond wasn't going to get away. He had big plans for her—and she wasn't going to be able to bat her eyelashes, jiggle her cleavage, or wiggle her ass into his good graces.

It had been quite a relief to find her unarmed beneath her skirt—unarmed except for an incredible pair of long, sleek, bare legs that Dolan couldn't quite get out of his mind. He wasn't sure what he would have done if she'd pulled a knife or a gun on him. He'd never had to fend off a woman before—most of his life had been spent doing just the opposite.

They passed through a canopy of thick Douglas firs and rode into a small clearing that brought the bright sun directly into their faces. He rubbed his eyes with his grimy leather glove and stretched out his tense back. Lack of sleep over the past few days had definitely caught up to him. But by supper time he'd be in Pine Oaks, and he was looking forward to getting some much-needed rest before heading out on a two-day trip to Sacramento. Considering the company he'd have, it was bound to be one hell of an interesting journey.

Realizing that his prisoner hadn't said a word since they'd mounted up twenty minutes before, Dolan glanced behind him to be sure she was still there. She was fidgeting in her saddle while looking closely into the thick forest surrounding them. "You jump from that horse and I'll tie you to it," he warned.

Her head came up, and stray wisps of dark gold hair

caught in her long lashes as she stared at him with startled green eyes. "I . . . I wasn't thinking of jumping. I . . ." She gave him a confused look. "Where, exactly, are we?"

Her gaze sank into his, soft and compelling, and Dolan actually found himself stung by a sharp twinge of guilt. Holy Christ, he was more tired than he thought. He turned forward, reminding himself that this woman was deception incarnate—that she usually carried a derringer in one garter belt, and a knife tucked down the other, and wasn't opposed to using either weapon.

This in mind, Dolan took a deep breath to lift the weight of guilt settling over his conscience.

"Are . . ." She cleared her throat. "Are you going to . . . to tell me why you're doing this?"

"End the bewildered act already, lady." It was really beginning to grate on his already raw nerves.

"Could . . . could you just tell me how long I was unconscious?"

Now that was certainly an interesting way to describe a nap. "Apparently just long enough," he replied dryly. Long enough for him to catch up with her anyway.

"My memory is so . . . so muddled. . . ."

Rose Diamond? Muddled? The idea was almost laughable, but Dolan managed to restrain himself. Better she think him brooding and dangerous for the time being. "Just keep your eyes and your thoughts straight ahead of you."

"It looks as if we're out in the middle of nowhere."

But looks could be deceiving. She was perfect evidence of that fact: dazzling to the eye, deceptive to the bone.

"Where are we going?"

"Sacramento." Dolan half expected her to put two

and two together at that point, but she didn't—or at least she didn't let on that she did.

"And . . . how much longer until we get there?"

"Three days." She let out a sharp gasp that drew his attention back to her. She was now looking decidedly pale as she clung to her saddle horn. "Did you have somewhere else you needed to be?" he added.

"Three days on . . . on *horseback*?"

"Would you rather walk?"

"Couldn't you maybe . . . steal us a truck? I'm . . ." She looked down at the animal beneath her. "I'm afraid I'm not very good at these things."

Dolan smirked to himself. He figured he was handling things pretty well if she was stooping to babbling gibberish to keep him off balance.

"Listen Mr. . . . Mr.—"

He returned his attention to the trail ahead of him. "The name's Dolan. Dolan Kincaid."

"Mr. Kincaid," she began calmly, as if speaking to a rabid dog. "Wh-whatever economic or . . . or social crisis have brought you to this point, I . . . I'm sure help can be found for you. Kidnapping me is certainly not the answer. In fact . . . it'll only make things worse for you in the end."

Dolan closed his eyes and tried to shut out the sound of her pointless efforts to sway him. Tonight. Tonight he would get some rest. . . .

"I'm sure you're feeling . . . desperate and . . . and confused."

So now *he* was the one supposedly confused? He focused on the soft bed that awaited him and the steamy hot meal. . . .

"B-but before this unfortunate situation gets out of

hand I think . . . we should head for the nearest town and find you some help."

He broke into a smile, which only the trees in front of him could see, and opened his eyes. "But we *are* headed for the nearest town."

"We are?" she asked, surprise keying up her voice.

"Yep. And we're both going to have a good night's sleep." Well, his would likely be better than hers; he'd heard that dirty straw ticking and rats tended to keep a person awake.

"Then . . . then maybe that would be the perfect time to go to the authorities," she said carefully.

"Absolutely."

"Absolutely?"

"I fully intend to go to the authorities with you, Miss Diamond."

"Who?"

"Who what?"

"You . . . you just called me Miss . . . Diamond."

"Uh huh."

"That isn't my name."

"Really? And what is it today?" When he'd tracked her to Mariposa she'd been using the name Lily White—interesting, if a bit contrary to the facts. He was sure she had a whole pocketful of interesting aliases, any one of which he was certain she'd employ at the slightest opportunity to annoy him.

"It's Jane Baker."

Despite himself, Dolan burst out laughing. "Well there's a plain, ordinary name if I've ever heard one." He glanced back at her. She was frowning. "I guess no one would ever expect a plain old Jane to have any kind of dubious reputation."

Dolan was completely unprepared for her responding expression of innocent confusion. Her wide green eyes actually grew moist, and he was all at once overcome with a sensation of such incredible remorse that he almost ended his scheme right then and there.

It was the oversimplified clothing she was wearing, he told himself. It made her seem timid—harmless. And her hair, tight and pulled back, made her look like a blasted schoolmarm.

He returned his attention to the trail ahead of him. "How about we just stick with Rose so neither one of us gets confused?"

"Rose?" she repeated weakly.

"Yeah. Rose. Your name *du jour.*"

"But my name isn't Rose." She'd said that lie without the slightest hint of deception in her quavering voice, and he didn't know whether to be impressed or outraged. "It's Jane. I was named after my grandmother."

"Well, I hope she wore the name better," he grumbled spitefully. Hell, for all he knew Jane really *was* her name—he certainly doubted it was Rose Diamond. But, for all intents and purposes, Rose Diamond was what he intended to call her for the duration of their trip.

She remained silent for a few moments, probably thinking of another tack to take to drive him crazy, while Dolan continued to fight with his own conflicting emotions. He'd been warned that she was a force to be reckoned with, nothing to take lightly, that man and beast alike tended to bow to her slightest whim. But he'd never dreamed she'd be so lovely, so harmless in appearance.

"So is it agreed, Mr. Kincaid?"

"Is what agreed?" he replied, moodily.

She cleared her throat—something, he was realizing, she did whenever she was attempting to seem nervous. "That we head straight for the authorities when we reach the next town."

He grunted satirically. Was she completely serious? "Your wish is my command."

"Then . . . you'll release me to the local authorities?" Dolan was impressed with the way she could make her voice quaver whenever she spoke, as if for one moment the infamous Rose Diamond could ever be afraid of anyone or anything. Any minute now she was bound to revert into the woman she was rumored to be and start screeching his ears off—making demands, throwing around blatant threats. He swore to himself that the first malicious thing out of her mouth was going to earn her a gag.

"Mr. Kincaid?" she prompted when he didn't immediately respond.

"Absolutely," he replied to her question. "We'll arrive in Pine Oaks in time for supper, although I can't guarantee you'll eat when we get there," he added, just for effect.

"You can't?"

"I'm not in charge of the jail."

There was a moment's pause, a moment in which Dolan imagined quite a look of horror had come over her face. Despite all her many escapades, Rose Diamond had yet to spend a single second in a jail cell. She was just too damn good at manipulating lawmen out of their determination—and, he strongly suspected, their pants.

"The *jail?*" she repeated weakly.

"That's where you'll be spending the night." She let

out a screech of horror that made Dolan turn in his saddle just in time to see her fall backward off her horse.


Nelson was absolutely frantic.

She was gone. She was *simply gone.* Jane Baker had completely disappeared from the face of the earth.

Any moment now he expected Stella to come storming into his office demanding to know how in heaven's name he could lose one measly little client. Was Miss Baker really so much for him to look after? Perhaps *Vikings* would be large enough for him to keep track of?

Nelson groaned as a faint shudder shook down through his spine. He had to find her. *Where the great blazes could she be?!*

The buzzer on his desk rattled, and he flew forward and slapped the button. "*Yes?*"

"Sir, I believe we've found her."

"Yes? Yes?!"

"There was apparently a mix-up on her return, sir—"

"All right, *woman,* get *on* with it! Where, in God's name, is she?!"

"1890."

Nelson paused and cocked his head at the intercom. "I beg your pardon."

"She's in 1890, sir, in the nineteenth century."

Nelson fell back into his chair and closed his eyes. He once again went over in his mind the steps he had taken to send Miss Baker back, and let out an unbelieving groan. He could see it now: great hulking men towering over him, laughing at his clothing and his puny muscles, refusing to believe that they were dead, let alone in a place called heaven, and his only armor would be a thin clipboard and a number two pencil.

"Sir? Would you like her coordinates fed to your terminal?"

"Yes," Nelson croaked. As if the coordinates would do him a bit of good. Jane Baker's soul was in another time, another place, and he had no idea how to get her back home.

# 4

*This time Jane's unexpected fall* simply knocked the wind out of her.

And thank heavens for that. She hated to imagine what her maniacal kidnapper might have done had she been knocked unconscious again. He probably would have shot her right then and there. The man was *completely* out of his mind, babbling about trials and hangings. And now he was threatening that she'd be spending the night in jail!

"*Jail?!*" she shouted up at him from where she was now lying, spread-eagled, on the ground.

He leaned on the pommel of his saddle and glowered down at her from beneath the wide brim of his dark cowboy hat. "Jail, Miss Diamond. Tonight you will be sleeping on a cot in a jail cell. I suggest you get used to the idea."

Get used to the idea? What twisted police station would allow this maniac to throw her in jail?

"Mr. Kincaid, you are obviously—"

"Lady," he interrupted sharply, "just get back on your goddamn horse."

Jane clenched her jaw and glared at him for a moment before looking straight up at the horse in question. She dreaded climbing back up there. Horsemanship didn't come naturally to her, and, if her kidnapper didn't kill her, another nasty fall off this animal just might. But Mr. Dolan Kincaid had already proven earlier that he would settle for nothing less than her total capitulation, so she sat up, slowly.

"I don't suppose it would make any difference if I told you I've never ridden a horse before?"

His answer was a bland stare.

"I didn't think so," she grumbled. He obviously wasn't going to be happy until she was dead, one way or another. "Maybe I'll take you up on that offer to tie me to the saddle. It might just help," she added to herself.

"What, and ruin all these wonderful theatrics of yours?"

Jane gave him a startled look. "You don't think I fell off this horse on purpose?"

He leaned back, his saddle creaking beneath him, and squinted up at the bright sky. "What I think is that you're wasting your breath and my time."

Jane gritted her teeth and reached for the saddle stirrup dangling in front of her. With a strong pull, she tried hoisting herself to her feet. But the horse didn't appreciate her effort and sidestepped, planting a heavy hoof on her skirt. As a result, Jane only made it about four inches off the ground before she could rise no farther.

She glared down at the impeding hoof and struggled in midair for a moment before finally plopping back down to earth with a disgruntled groan. Though afraid of what she would see, she chanced a glance at her kidnapper.

Dolan Kincaid's bland stare hadn't changed, and he didn't appear at all inclined to help her. And Jane wasn't about to ask.

She gave her skirt a frantic tug, but couldn't budge the strong material out from beneath the horse's weight. She tried coaxing the animal, in her best librarian voice, to please move over a step or two, but it only craned its neck around, stared dully at her, and snorted, wetly, in her direction.

For one brief, obtuse moment Jane actually considered bursting into tears. She'd seen women in movies use that ploy successfully a number of times. Maybe playing on her abductor's tender side would work in her favor. But then she remembered what a horrible actress she was. And besides, she sincerely doubted her abductor *had* a tender side.

In a last-ditch effort, she braced her feet against the horse's impeding leg, and pushed with all her might. "*Geettt offff,*" she gritted out.

But the animal wasn't moving for all the oats in Oklahoma. With a defeated groan, she lay on her back and closed her eyes.

"Oh for Christ's sake."

She heard the leather creak of Mr. Kincaid's saddle as he dismounted, but she kept her eyes squeezed tight, not wanting to see the disgust she'd already heard in his voice mirrored in his steel-blue gaze. Yes, she was pathetic—she was also pointless and ineffectual. But she certainly didn't need a cold, heartless criminal rubbing it in.

The stubborn horse snorted, and she felt a faint tug on her skirt. Then she felt the strong, sure grip of her kidnapper's hands slip beneath her underarms and haul her to her feet. Embarrassed by her innate clumsiness and characteristic ineptitude, and irritated that he'd been forced to help her when it was apparently the last thing in the world he'd wanted to do, Jane stumbled back from his grasp. "Thank you," she muttered.

"You're just putting off the inevitable," he replied.

"I did not fall intentionally," Jane replied, barely keeping her tone in check as she batted dried clumps of grass and clods of dirt from her skirt. She couldn't imagine why he would think she'd try to break her neck on purpose.

"Right."

And his sarcastic attitude was really beginning to get on her nerves. *She* was the injured party here. *She* was the one who'd been kidnapped, unconscious, from her home and dragged out here into the middle of the wilderness. *She* was the one who should be hostile and disdainful.

"I may be a bit uncoordinated," she said tightly, "but I assure you that when I *choose* to get down from this hairy brontosaurus it will *not* be headfirst."

"From what I hear, Miss Diamond . . ." he paused, suddenly taking a strange, keen interest in the left side of her neck, "nothing you do is unintentional."

"My name is Jane Baker," she said, rubbing self-consciously at the spot on her neck that was so avidly holding his interest. "And just about everything I *do* is unintentional."

He reached for her, and Jane quickly stepped backward. But she underestimated his reach and he took a tight grip on her shoulders and pulled her close. She gasped as he shoved her head sideways and moved his face in as if he were about to take a chunk out of her neck, vampire-style. Frankly, Jane wouldn't have put it past the strange man. He rubbed at the side of her neck with his leather-gloved fingers as if looking for a suitable vein.

"What . . . um . . . What exactly are you doing?" Jane asked hesitantly, uncomfortable with him standing so close.

"Where the hell is it?" He cocked her head in the other direction and examined the right side of her neck.

"What?" Jane asked, confused once again by his odd behavior.

"The rose tattoo on the side of your neck."

Jane shook her head. "I don't have a tattoo."

He gave her a thoughtful scowl. "Apparently not."

Jane was relieved when he let go of her and headed back to his horse. He seemed suddenly disconcerted, creating what she thought might be a prime moment for her to attempt to reason with him.

"You know, you're lucky I didn't break my neck falling off that horse, or . . . or you'd be facing a murder charge along with everything else."

He glanced back at her. "Everything else?"

Faced with his intense blue stare yet again, Jane almost lost what little nerve she'd managed to gather. "K-kidnapping for starters," she went on bravely.

"Kidnapping?" He nudged his hat back on his head and chuckled. "Well, I am just *dyin'* to hear the logic behind that."

His sudden and, in her opinion, misplaced humor, was annoying to say the least. "You stole me right off my sidewalk—and right out from under the nose of Mrs. Hatterly," she accused. "That woman can smell a crime a half a mile away, so don't you think for one *minute* that you're going to get away with *any* of this."

"Mrs. Hatterly?" he repeated, folding his arms over his chest. "Would that be the busty woman with all the lipstick? Or the redhead with the Colt .45?"

Jane blinked. *Busty? Redheaded?* Since her recent bout with liver cancer old Mrs. Hatterly was as bald as a cue ball and weighed all of about sixty pounds. "I beg your pardon?"

"Friends of yours I met in Mariposa. They were very pleased to inform me that I'd missed you, that you'd scampered out of town the day before I arrived."

Jane shook her head slowly. She had no friends in Mariposa, California—she'd never even set foot in the town.

"Fortunately for me you left a very angry bunch of men in your wake as well, men who were more than happy to tell me the direction you'd ridden. They claimed you cheated them out of fifty dollars in a game of poker. Only fifty, Rose? You must be slipping."

Assuming that laughing at the criminally insane was probably impolite, not to mention downright dangerous, Jane refrained. "I barely know how to play Go Fish, Mr. Kincaid, let alone *cheat* my way through a game of poker. Those men were obviously referring to someone else."

He smirked. "Right."

"Yes. That *is* right." Good lord. Saloons? Poker games? Busty, red-haired women with guns? Forget therapy, this man needed a padded cell! "I have never played a game of poker in my life," she insisted, determined to get through to his saner side—even though she was beginning to doubt he had one.

"Right."

"*Stop saying that!*" she snapped.

His eyes narrowed on her, making her heart thud heavily in her chest. "I knew this little docile and pathetic act of yours was bound to dissolve eventually."

"*What* in *God's name* are you *talking* about?!" Frustration was once again beginning to override Jane's cautious side. "I am *not* Rose Diamond! You have to believe me!"

"Lady, I don't have to believe one good goddamn thing. And as far as believing *you* goes, I wouldn't believe you if you told me the grass was green."

"But you don't even *know* me!"

"Ah, but I know all about you. Who hasn't heard of California's notorious lady gambler and all her many exploits?"

Exploits? It was safe to say that Jane Baker had never had an "exploit" in her life. And so it was becoming very apparent to her that Mr. Dolan Kincaid had made a serious blunder. "I don't quite know how to break this to you, Mr. Kincaid, but you have obviously kidnapped the wrong person."

The unreasonable man actually laughed at her. "I'm sure that's exactly what you hoped I'd believe when I stumbled across you in that meadow all dressed up in those dowdy clothes."

Jane looked down at herself: her skirt was grass- and ink-stained; her white, pin-striped blouse had a dark smudge across the front where he'd grabbed her with his dirty gloved hands. She shoved a loose strand of hair back from her face, knowing she had to look ten times worse than normal.

"Did you really think you could fool me by dressing in those plain clothes and pulling back your hair? Face it, Miss Diamond, you've met your match. I've tracked enough men and dealt with enough outlaws to know all the tricks. You can't distract me, you can't con me, and you can't sweet-talk me. So for *both* our sakes I suggest you give the hell up."

Jane didn't know what to say. He was so deeply enmeshed in his own delusion that he couldn't see what was standing right in front of him. She was a plain, unremarkable librarian—not a lying, cheating, poker-playing vamp.

He turned for his horse while Jane remained where she was, fighting a feeling of hopelessness. She would have to be strong if she hoped to survive whatever this situation had in store for her. She couldn't let this man make her crazy. *He* was the only lunatic here. And soon he would be captured and made to pay for the emotional distress he was putting her through.

She would not lose her composure again. She would not let anything he did or said upset her. She would stay very, very calm.

And she was fully prepared to stick with that plan of action—until a bullet went whizzing past her head.


The first shot *zinged!* between Dolan and his prisoner and embedded in a fir tree a few yards away. It also pulled a scream out of Rose Diamond loud enough to wake the dead.

He dove for her, dragging her to the ground behind the shelter of a thick pine. To her credit, Rose didn't fight him as he shoved her down onto her stomach in the grass and pine needles; to his, he didn't crack her over the head when she continued to scream in his ear.

"Christ! Would you shut the hell up!" He yanked his gun out of his holster.

Bullets were flying all around them, zinging off rocks and ricocheting into trees. One came particularly close to Dolan's head; it whined past his ear, and tore a hole in the broad leaf of a nearby rhododendron. "Shit," he blurted.

"W-what's happening?" Miss Diamond stammered. Dolan had to give her credit; to someone less knowledgeable about her character she would have seemed shocked and out of breath. "Who's shooting at us?"

As if she didn't know.

The wild shooting finally stopped, and Dolan thumbed back the hammer on his gun as he cautiously peeked around the pine tree. He saw movement in the undergrowth ten yards away, but couldn't make out any definitive targets.

"Would you please tell me what's going on?!" Miss Diamond cried.

"Welcome to your rescue attempt," he muttered. He took a bead on a likely target and fired.

The loud *bang!* of his gun going off made his prisoner cry out in alarm again.

"Just settle back, Miss Diamond. This'll only take a minute."

"But . . . if they're *rescuing* me, then why are they *shooting* at me?"

"Because they're idiots. Goddamn it." He couldn't get a clear shot through all the trees. "I was hoping I'd seen the last of these two when you sent them back to throw me off your trail," he said, shoving aside the long fronds of a fern. "I don't suppose they told you that I heard them coming from a half-mile away and was gone before they finally managed to stumble onto my camp."

Rose didn't answer, and, realizing she'd become noticeably quiet, Dolan glanced down at her. She was staring off into space, looking very pale and slightly dazed.

Rose Diamond . . . dazed? Dolan became instantly suspicious. But before he could react, the damn woman scrambled to her feet, screaming, "Help! Help!"

Dolan lunged for her, grabbing one of her ankles and hauling her back to the ground just as more bullets began to fly through the air around them. The battle with his prisoner didn't end there however. She started flailing like a cornered wildcat, striking out with her hands and feet. She kicked him square between the eyes before he was able to climb on top of her and shove her, facedown, into the pine needles once again.

"No fair changing sides in the middle of the game, Miss Diamond," he stated, out of breath from their struggle. "Now, I suggest you keep your pretty little head down because Barney and Cleavus aren't exactly crack shots. They couldn't hit the broad side of an elephant at two and a half paces."

"Please," she cried, her voice muffled by the ground. "Please give yourself up!"

"I never give up, lady. Not myself, and not my prisoners."

She seemed to freeze in that moment. She turned her head and stared sideways at him with wide, green eyes. "*Prisoners*? Are you saying you've done this kind of thing *before*?"

Dolan ducked as another wild bullet went flying past and drove into the trunk of the tree behind them. He gave her a twisted smile. "You still respect me, don'cha?"

She looked completely horror-struck. "You . . . are a very . . . horrible . . . man."

Dolan leaned to one side, lightening his weight on her slender back. "Coming from you, Miss Diamond," he replied, peeking around the trunk of the tree once more, "I'll take that as a compliment."

And then the shooting stopped as suddenly as it had begun. Dolan rose up a little to make sure his opponents weren't trying to sneak around behind him. In his five years on the job, the outlaws Barney Rollins and Cleavus Coltrain had generally been more of a nuisance than anything else. But in the past week they'd proved very loyal to Rose Diamond by getting in his way more than a few times.

"Mr. Kincaid, please," Rose Diamond begged from beneath him, "*please* let me go. What can you hope to *gain* from all this?"

"Intense satisfaction," Dolan replied distractedly.

And then the high-keyed, panicked voice of Barney Rollins called out to him. "Let her go, Kincaid. And maybe we'll letcha walk away from here alive!"

Considering Barney had the reputation of shooting his own foot before hitting his target, Dolan figured he'd take his chances. "You boys run along now," he called back, "before you really start to make me mad."

"You heard them," Rose Diamond said to him, "they won't shoot you if you let me go."

With these two, getting shot was the least of Dolan's worries. He just didn't appreciate the bother of yet another delay.

*"You got ten seconds, Kincaid!"*

"Ten seconds till what?" Dolan muttered as he

checked the cylinder on his gun. "Ten seconds before they start shooting each other?"

"*You'll never make it to Sacramento!*" Cleavus Coltrain called out. "*We aim to see to that!*"

"Well, I'm just shakin' all over." As if this whole situation weren't difficult enough, he had these two idiots to contend with. It was like having two pesky mosquitoes buzzing around his head all day.

He looked off into the underbrush again, chose his aim carefully, and fired. This time he was rewarded with a loud, echoing yelp.

"I'm hit! I'm hit, Barn! Ahhhhh, I'm hit!"

"Stop your wailin'," was Barney's hissed response. "You're screamin' like a little girl."

"Ahhhh, it hurts! It burns! I'm dyin'!"

"Lemme see. Ah, it's just a little nick in the arm."

"I'm crippled, scarred for life! He shot off my gun arm, Barn. My gun arm! Ahhh, it hurts like the very devil!"

"Quit yer whinin' and get on yer horse!"

A few seconds later two horses went crashing through the forest and toward a distant cattle trail. "We'll be back for ya, Miss Rose!" Barney Rollins called. "Don'chu worry none!"

Dolan watched them ride away, and then rolled off his prisoner's back. He reholstered his gun and sat down against the tree. "You can get up now."

Rose pushed herself up to a sitting position beside him. She was covered from head to toe with grass and pine needles, which clung to her clothes and dangled from her disheveled hair. She pushed the wispy mess back from her face, and gave him a haunted look. There were tears shimmering in her eyes.

"Ah, don't start cryin'." There was nothing he hated more than dealing with a hysterical woman.

She dashed at the tears before they could fall down her cheeks, which were pink from the hot sun. Freckles were beginning to come out in faint patches across the bridge of her nose, and Dolan found himself wishing he'd brought along an extra hat. How could this woman, who had a reputation for being hard and brash, seem so incredibly fragile? She was either quite the actress, or he was quite the fool. He preferred to believe the former.

"Well. That was certainly fun."

She gave him a harsh stare as tears continued to glisten on her thick lashes. "You have just *shot* a man, Mr. Kincaid. Is that *all* you have to say?"

"I didn't know I was supposed to make a speech."

"Didn't you hear them?" she demanded, her voice rising. "They are not going to let you get to Sacramento. There will be police cars, roadblocks—helicopters!"

"Really?" he responded dryly. She was back to talking gibberish again. "Well, then, I guess I better use my magic bubble to protect myself."

She took a deep breath. "Mr. Kincaid, you must know that you are caught up in a delusion."

"Really?"

"*Really,*" she repeated forcefully. "Why else would you be doing this?"

He hooded his eyes. Why else indeed. "Maybe I'm just incredibly desperate for company, and couldn't resist your rumored reputation with gentlemen."

She stared blankly at him. "Do I *look* as if I have a reputation with men?"

Dolan glanced over her messy hair, her dirty, tear-streaked face, her wrinkled, stained clothes, and was irritated that, all things considered, she was still a god-damn good-looking woman. She had classic features: large, round eyes, high, elegant cheekbones, a straight, narrow nose. And her lips were wide and full, perfectly kissable. The truth of the matter was, he was pretty damn attracted to her.

"Shit." He climbed to his feet, disgusted with himself. An attraction to a viper was the last thing he needed.

He took hold of her hand and hauled her to her feet. "Pine Oaks is only two hours away."

"Good," she said, brushing off her skirt. "Maybe someone there can talk some sense into you."

"I wouldn't count on that." He took her around the waist and lifted her back into her saddle.

"And why not?" she called after him as he headed for his own horse.

"Considering your past with Pine Oaks's marshal . . ." he said, mounting up.

"My past with him?" she asked. Dolan didn't miss the distinctly hopeful tone to her voice. "You mean I *know* him?"

"Oh, you two go way back."

"You mean he knows *Rose Diamond*."

Dolan gave her a sideways glance as he urged his horse up next to hers and took hold of her reins. "Very well."

"Wonderful." She lifted her dainty chin, and the sun glinted brightly in her green eyes. "Then he'll be able to tell you once and for all that I am *not* this Rose Diamond woman."

She seemed so confident, so sure of that fact, that Dolan actually paused and looked her over carefully for a moment. Certainly there could be no doubt of who she was. What other woman would be lying in a meadow, horseless, companionless, and thirty miles from the nearest town? She matched Rose Diamond's description exactly.

Ah, she was just trying to fool with his head. And as for that lack of a tattoo on the left side of her neck, wanted posters had been known to be wrong.

One thing was definitely for certain: in just a few short hours Marshal Jack Ford would put an end to the question of her identity once and for all. And then Dolan could get down to the real business of why he'd gone to so much trouble to capture the country's finest lady cardsharp.

**5**

*Two hours later,* Jane was brought to a halt outside the city limits of Pine Oaks, California. She'd been riding behind Dolan Kincaid for what felt like days.

The sun was setting in the distance, a deep orange ball of fire hanging over the tops of the pines. She'd managed to stay mounted since her last embarrassing fall, but after spending all day in the saddle, all she wanted was out of it. She was tired, dirty, and practically numb from the waist down.

She squinted through the thick dust in the air and shifted her sore bottom in her saddle. The city before her looked lacking, to say the very least: lacking in cars, paved roads, skyscrapers, malls, even 7-Elevens. Pine Oaks, California, appeared to be a shadow of a town at best, and, if not for the twenty or so people milling around the main street, Jane would have thought the place completely deserted. And what was with all the horses? she thought as she was slowly led through the center of town. They were everywhere, being ridden, or tied to one of many hitching posts that were lined up along the wide, dirt street like guardrails. Jane gawked as an old-fashioned wagon rumbled past her pulled by two gigantic draft horses. And she gawked even harder at the huge, scruffy man driving the contraption.

She gave Dolan Kincaid a sidelong glance, wondering what he thought of all this, and found that he didn't seem particularly bothered by what he was seeing. The two of them had spoken little since Jane's "rescue attempt" earlier—she felt that any efforts toward conversation on her part would be a serious waste of time considering that the man refused to believe a single word that came out of her mouth.

She'd decided instead to save her breath and lay all of her hopes on the marshal of Pine Oaks. If he truly did know Rose Diamond, then he would be able to put this whole misunderstanding to rest once and for all. But now Jane was beginning to wonder about any marshal who lived in this odd little town.

"I thought you said you were taking me to a city," she said to Mr. Kincaid as their horses carried them at a rocking gait down what appeared to be the main street of town.

"This is the city of Pine Oaks."

"*This* is a *city*?" she replied. It didn't even have a gas station—which certainly explained why everyone was riding horses. Her hopes of a hot bath and a nice soft bed for the night were beginning to look pretty slim.

A nearby door slammed, and she glanced around at the buildings on either side of her: old-style saloons, hat and gun shops, blacksmith and livery stables, even a bathhouse across from a place called the Grand Hotel— which looked anything *but* grand.

The people all paused to stare as she rode past. The

women were all wearing old-style dresses, with shawls around their shoulders and bonnets covering their hair. The men wore pants, suspenders, jackets, with either western-style hats with wide brims, or old-fashioned bowlers.

And each and every one of them was armed to the teeth.

Some of them simply wore pistols in holsters on their hips, in the style of Mr. Kincaid, while others casually carried rifles slung over their shoulders as if the weapons were merely an accessory.

"What kind of place is this?" Jane finally asked.

"It's called a respectable town, Miss Diamond. But I can understand why it would seem so foreign to you."

"Well, it looks like a *dangerous* town to me."

"Only dangerous for the disreputable." He gave her a dry smile. "I'm sure you have nothing to worry about."

Jane ignored that comment as he led her to a one-story, whitewashed building with the words TOWN MARSHAL painted in black letters above the door. He dismounted, and wrapped his reins around a thick hitching post, while Jane stayed on her horse, her attention on the office door, waiting for the marshal to emerge and end this entire horrendous ordeal.

"Evening," Mr. Kincaid said, nodding to someone behind her.

Jane turned in her saddle to find that a small crowd had followed them to the marshal's office. She smiled reluctantly at the people. None of them smiled back, and a tight lump of apprehension rose up in her throat.

"You folks need something?" Mr. Kincaid asked.

"Is that who I think it is, sonny?" an older gentleman with thin gray hair demanded, pointing a gnarled finger at Jane.

Mr. Kincaid nudged his hat back on his head, revealing his sharp blue eyes. "Well, now, I guess that all depends on who you think she is."

"That there is Rose Diamond," the old man piped up.

Jane blinked at him in astonishment. "I most certainly am not."

"This lady claims her name is Jane," Mr. Kincaid replied.

The older man made a disgusted sound through his fleshy lips. "That there is Rose Diamond. Plain as the nose on my face."

And it was rather plain. Short, flat, not much to look at, at all.

A scruffy young man standing beside the old man turned to the crowd. "Hey, everybody!" he called out. "It's Rose Diamond! She's Rose Diamond!"

"I am not Rose Diamond!" Jane protested.

"Yes, you is," the old man declared. "Seen you in San Francisco once. She's her. She's Rose Diamond."

"Whoowee," someone else called out. "Rose Diamond sure is somethin', ain't she?"

Jane gritted her teeth. These people were not helping her cause. "For the last time, I am *not*—"

She was cut short when Mr. Kincaid reached up and lifted her off her horse. "Come on," he said, setting her on the dusty boards of the sidewalk. "You can convince 'em you're the good fairy some other time."

"This entire town is crazy," Jane insisted, stumbling slightly as he guided her through the narrow doorway of the marshal's office. "I am *not* Rose Diamond."

"Hello, Rose."

Jane stopped cold. The room was lit with two kerosene lanterns spaced ten feet apart on the far wall, which illuminated a potbellied stove, a fully stocked gun rack, and a large oak desk. A dark-haired man sitting behind the desk was smiling lopsidedly at her. "It's been a long time," the man said, rising to his feet.

After the long, complicated day she'd had, Jane actually found herself staring hard at the marshal of Pine Oaks, trying to determine if she really did know him. After only a few seconds she was sure that she'd never met him before in her life. "I have no idea who you are," she replied confidently.

"Ah, now that's no way to greet an old friend, Rose." He came around the desk and smiled at Dolan Kincaid. "Kincaid. You look like ten miles of bad road."

Mr. Kincaid grunted. "It's been a long week."

"And you—" the marshal said, turning his attention back to Jane.

He was very tall, and very broad through the chest. He and Mr. Kincaid were roughly the same size, and as they stood together, towering over her, Jane felt vastly outnumbered and seriously overwhelmed.

"You, Rose, look just as good as you did the last time I saw you," the marshal continued. "Even with your hair atangle and four inches of trail dust on you."

How in God's name could he say that with a straight face? Jane thought frantically. "I do not know you, sir, and you *certainly* don't know me. I am *not* Rose Diamond." Were these people intentionally trying to drive her insane?

The marshal gave Dolan Kincaid a questioning glance. "She's not?"

"Ah, she's been spouting that line all day. Insists I've got the wrong woman."

The marshal grunted. "Now, why am I not surprised. I told you she'd try anything to get away from ya."

"Yeah, she's led me on quite a merry chase for the past week."

"Hell, I'm surprised you caught up with her, *period*."

Jane was clenching her teeth to keep from screaming in frustration. They were talking about her as if she weren't even in the room. "Who are you people?" she finally blurted out. "What do you want with me?" This was obviously some sort of conspiracy between friends.

Neither man even bothered to glance her way. "I take it she's been keepin' you on your toes," the marshal said.

"Let's just say I could really use a good night's sleep."

"Kristen's makin' chicken and dumplings for dinner."

Dolan Kincaid broke into a broad grin. "God love the woman."

"*Excuse* me!" Jane screeched. Her normally mild temper was really being tested—and all this talk about food was making her empty stomach hurt. "Would one of you *please* answer my questions?"

The men finally turned her way. "She seems to be taking all of this a whole lot better than I imagined," the marshal said.

"Yeah, well, don't let her composure fool you. She's not at all happy about being caught. She tried ditching her horse last night just to throw me off track."

Jane gasped at the lie. "I did no such thing! He found me *unconscious* just this morning!"

"Unconscious?" the marshal repeated. He arched a dark brow at Dolan Kincaid.

"Unconscious my ass. After searching all morning for her I finally found her taking a nap in a meadow."

Jane's mind was spinning. It was difficult keeping track of the conversation when it was becoming so convoluted with Mr. Kincaid's delusions. "Marshal," she pleaded, "you have to help me. This man is completely insane. I was *unconscious* when he kidnapped me off my sidewalk—"

"Kidnapped her?" the marshal interrupted, turning once again to Dolan Kincaid.

Mr. Kincaid crossed his arms and smiled crookedly. "And she claims I won't get away with it."

The marshal broke into laughter. "My God, you *have* had your hands full. I've only been listening to her for two minutes and my head's *already* hurtin'."

Jane closed her eyes and said a silent prayer. She'd been abducted by a kook. Brought to Kookville. And was now being introduced to *Officer* Kook. Things were going from bad to worse.

"Okay, Rose—"

"My name is not Rose, you bumbling fool!" she snapped. She didn't care anymore that they were each wearing guns—let them shoot her and put her out of her misery!

"Oh, that's another thing," Mr. Kincaid said calmly. "She claims her name is really Jane Barker."

"*Baker*!" Jane corrected. "My name is Jane *Baker*!"

The marshal smiled and shook his head. "Rose, you and I have known each other for a lotta years, so don't try pullin' any of this crap on me."

Jane gave him a shocked look. "I have never met you before in my life. *Please, please* just let me *go*. I promise I won't tell anyone about this—I won't breathe a word. I'm just a simple librarian from Littleville, California, for God's sake." Her throat went tight with tears. "I just want to go home. I need to water my plant. I'm sure I left my back door unlocked. And . . . and I don't have anybody to open the library tomorrow."

The two men stared at her in silence for a moment, and Jane actually thought that maybe her emotional plea was getting through to them. But then Dolan Kincaid shook his head. "She's amazing."

"Always said she should be on the stage," the marshal agreed.

"Let's get her into a cell before she breaks into song." The marshal turned and lifted a heavy ring of keys from his desk, which he then tossed to Jane's abductor. "After you," Mr. Kincaid said to her, indicating that he wanted her to walk ahead of him down the narrow hallway at the back of the room.

Jane's shoulders drooped. It would do her little good to refuse. It seemed she would be spending the night in a jail cell after all.

She bravely walked forward and preceded Dolan Kincaid down the hallway. She passed old photographs on the walls, a lit lantern, and an old wagon wheel hung around a small circular mirror for decoration.

There were old-fashioned wanted posters hanging on the walls as well, and one in particular happened to catch Jane's eye. She came to a screeching halt, which forced Mr. Kincaid to bump solidly into her back.

"Oh my God," she breathed.

She moved closer, staring hard at the sketch of the woman with long, flowing hair. She was seeing *her* eyes, *her* nose, *her* mouth. The sketch was a perfect likeness of herself.

She was apparently wanted . . . *dead or alive.*


The damn fool woman had passed out colder than a dead fish. Hell, she was lucky he'd been standing so close at hand, or she'd have whacked her head on the wall behind her.

Dolan had then been forced to lift her up into his arms and carry her into her cell. He suspected that this was just another ruse on Rose's part, another ploy to put him off guard, but that suspicion had pretty much been dispelled when the woman had dangled in his arms like a wet noodle.

She'd come around just as he was laying her on her cot. But instead of cutting loose with another round of "I'm not Rose," she'd simply lain there, staring at him with liquid green eyes.

That was when Dolan had gotten a sense of just how tired and worn out he really was by the way that haunted stare of hers had pulled at his heart. The woman had absolutely no shame at all—and he, apparently, had no sense. He stood there, staring at her, wordless as she held him with her eyes. He probably wouldn't have moved the entire night long if Jack hadn't finally called to him from the front office. At that point Dolan had offered her a hasty "good night" and clanged her cell door shut, quickly making his exit. Orders were left with a deputy to fetch the prisoner some food from Kirkwood's Restaurant across the street, and then Dolan had followed Jack home for a decent meal and what he hoped would be a decent night's sleep.

"You look like hell," Jack said to him now from across a small pine table. It was two hours later, and Dolan was sitting in Jack's small kitchen drinking coffee after a delectable meal of chicken and dumplings.

He gave his friend a wry smile, still trying to get that frightened, doelike look of Rose Diamond's out of his uncooperative mind. "I feel like *shit*."

"Don't let her get to ya, Kincaid."

Dolan blinked at his friend's insight, and then smiled. "Ah, hell, I'm just tired. It's a lot easier bringing in men, ya know. If a man rubs me the wrong way, I just knock him silly and toss him over his saddle. And"—he laughed—"although I've dreamed of doing just that to Miss Rose Diamond several times in the past week, when I finally came across her in that meadow I just didn't quite have it in me."

Jack arched his dark, bushy brows and looked down into his coffee mug. "I warned ya she'd drive you half nuts. To tell the truth, I'm surprised she didn't tear ya to shreds."

"She's been surprisingly calm," Dolan said thoughtfully. "Listen, I know this is gonna sound crazy, but . . . could there be anything to what she's saying? Is it at all possible that I've got the wrong woman? I mean, there is that missing tattoo—"

"Well, she didn't have one four years ago when I knew her. It's obviously just a mistake on the poster. Relax, Kincaid. Unless Rose came up with a twin since last we met, that woman in my office tonight was the real thing."

"Then where's the vicious, vindictive, *dangerous* side of her you warned me so much about? She's a bit of a pain the neck, Jack, but hardly the spiteful she-devil you made her out to be."

"I also told you she was faithless. You can't trust the woman farther than you can spit, Kincaid—and that's stretching things. My guess is this is all a scheme on her part to throw you off balance. The confused and helpless female is a tough ploy for any man to ignore." Jack gave him a speculative look. "And, apparently, it's workin'."

Dolan didn't answer. It was true that Rose Diamond had gotten under his skin a bit, but he had things under control. Hell, Jack was right; he was being ridiculous. Of course he had the right woman. Who else could she be?

He smiled and grunted. "What the hell did she see in that wanted poster anyway?"

Jack grinned. "Probably didn't think it was very flattering. A bad portrait can make the hardiest female swoon."

"Get your feet off the table, Jack."

Jack Parrish, former shootist and stagecoach robber, immediately dropped his dirty boots to the floor as his wife, Kristen, seven months pregnant with their first child, came strolling into the kitchen. Dolan lifted his coffee cup to his mouth to hide his smirk. He never would have believed it if he hadn't seen it with his own eyes: The beast in Jack had been tamed.

Kristen smiled at them both as she passed by, heading for the sink to pump some water into a tin kettle. "And what have you two gentlemen got your heads together about in here?"

"Rose Dia—" Dolan got a swift kick under the table.

"Nothin' for you to worry about, honey," Jack quickly interjected, giving Dolan a subtle glare. "By the way, dinner was great. Wasn't it, Kincaid?"

"Oh. Yeah. Incredible."

But Kristen was too quick for both of them. She'd turned from the sink and honed in on that name like a bat diving for mosquitoes. "Rose Diamond?" she asked, her steady gaze on her husband. "Isn't she that card-playing, gun-toting saloon girl you used to know?"

Jack sighed. "That'd be her, honey."

He gave Dolan a thanks-so-much-friend look and

Dolan could only shrug an apology. How was he supposed to know what and what not to say around Kristen? Since Dolan had known the two of them, Kristen had pretty much been an integral part of Jack's life.

But Dolan supposed it wasn't so much keeping things from Kristen as keeping *Kristen* from *things.* The woman liked to be involved—damnedest thing Dolan had ever seen. She could outsmart, outshoot, and outstubborn half the men he knew. And she had a pretty damn powerful right hook to boot. He knew that firsthand.

She came forward and sat down on her husband's lap. Jack cradled her, and splayed a protective hand over her rounded abdomen. "So what's up with Rose?" she asked straight out. Kristen Ford had never been one to beat around the bush.

"Nothin' for you to worry about. Honest," Jack replied, giving her a soft kiss on the neck. Then he gave Dolan a look that said not to utter another word about it. And Dolan took that look seriously. Jack protected Kristen just as ferociously as she protected him. Dolan was glad these two people were on his side of the law.

But it hadn't always been that way.

Only a year ago, he'd been tracking Jack and his gang for the two-hundred-dollar bounties on their heads. Back then he couldn't even have imagined a day when he'd be sitting in Jack Parrish's kitchen, drinking coffee, and trying not to stare as Jack nuzzled his pregnant wife's neck. But since then Jack had given up crime for a badge, traded in his reputation for a wife, and changed his last name to Ford. And Jack, himself, would be the first one to admit that the reason behind his amazing metamorphosis was his tough-as-nails little wife.

It was just over a year ago that Dolan had stumbled upon the two of them outside Volcano, Nevada. He'd taken one look at Jack Parrish, weak and hobbling from a gunshot wound to the leg, and smiled at his own good fortune.

However, Dolan had made the serious mistake of underestimating the woman *with* the wanted outlaw.

Kristen had guarded Jack like a fierce mother bear. But she was such a little bitty thing that Dolan had laughed, and dismissed her. That was when she'd given him a real good taste of her hard right hook—and pulled the oddest-looking gun Dolan had ever seen out of her purse. Odd or not, the damn gun worked; she'd shot a hole clean through his hat to prove it.

After a lengthy discussion—in which Dolan had been tied securely to a tree—Kristen had actually convinced him that Jack Parrish had changed his ways, that he was ready to become a law-abiding citizen and pay back his debt to society.

Call it mercy, call it curiosity, hell, call it blind stupidity, Dolan had kissed two hundred dollars good-bye that day and had let Jack Parrish go free. Jack and Kristen Ford were now counted as his two closest friends.

"When you tell me not to worry, Jack, that's when I worry," Kristen replied.

"Rose Diamond is not our problem. She's Kincaid's. Right, Kincaid?"

Dolan nodded. "There's a hundred-dollar bounty on her head in Sacramento. I'm taking her in."

"Sacramento?" Kristen repeated, arching a blond brow. "Isn't that where that poker tournament takes place around this time every year? The one you've been scheming to be a part of for months? Hmmm. And Rose Diamond is reputed to be one of the best cardsharps in the country. The two things wouldn't have anything to do with each other, now, would they?"

Dolan, not knowing how to respond, drank down the last of his coffee.

Jack busted out laughing. "Give it up, Kincaid. You can't put anything past her. I've tried."

"Dolan, tell me you're not actually going to make a *deal* with that jezebel," Kristen demanded. "Jack, haven't you told him what kind of woman she is?"

"I tried to warn him, honey," Jack said, shaking his head. "But you know how stubborn he can be."

"Yeah," Kristen replied. "Especially when it comes to this poker tournament."

"We're talking about over thirty thousand dollars here," Dolan replied. "A chance like this doesn't come along every day. With that kind of money I can get my own ranch and quit this business. I could settle down. Isn't that what you two keep telling me to do?"

"But isn't there somebody else you could green stake?" Kristen asked. "What about that other guy you were telling us about, that . . . that Stinky Sue."

"Pinky Lou," Jack corrected.

Dolan sighed. "Pinky got caught cheating in a game down south last month and was shot right through his queen of hearts."

"Well, there has to be somebody else," Kristen demanded. "Somebody less likely than Rose Diamond to stab you in the back—literally!"

Dolan shook his head. "There's nobody else. It's Rose or it's nobody."

"Well, I cast my vote for the latter," Kristen replied. "You're crazy to trust that woman."

"Nobody said anything about trusting her," Dolan replied. "I'm merely attempting to invest in what could be a very profitable venture."

"Always the businessman," Jack said, grinning.

Kristen grunted and rolled her eyes. "Stubborn. You men are all alike." She hefted her cumbersome girth from her husband's lap and swaggered away.

"Ah, where ya goin', honey?" Jack called.

"In the living room," she snapped back. "To pray for a girl!"

Both men grinned at her retort and settled back into their chairs. "You've got a handful there, Jack."

"Don't I know it. But she does have a point, Kincaid." He stretched out his long legs and put his feet back up on the table. "So what's the big plan? How do you propose to get Rose Diamond, a woman who'd rather shoot her own mother than help another living soul, go in with you in a poker tourney?"

Dolan smiled confidently. "By appealing to her survival instincts."

Jack's brows arched in curiosity.

"My friend," Dolan said, leaning forward, "by the time I'm finished with the lovely Miss Diamond it won't even occur to her that she's helping me win a sizable fortune. She'll be too busy scrambling to save her own neck."

**6**

*Jane was finally beginning to understand.* She
hadn't been kidnapped. Dolan Kincaid wasn't crazy.
These people thought she was Rose Diamond—under-
standably so, considering the spooky resemblance—and
Miss Rose Diamond was wanted. Dead or alive.

She was sitting on a thin, lumpy mattress on a narrow,
wooden cot that was pushed against the cement wall of an
eight-by-ten cell. The small room was illuminated by a lit
lantern hanging on the wall outside the sturdy iron bars
that made up the front of her cell. She was alone. The
room was quiet except for the subtle snores of Deputy
Tuggle, who'd obviously fallen asleep in the front office.

She stared down at the greasy plate of fried chicken
and potatoes on the floor at her feet. Her dinner. The
only food she'd been offered all day. But she didn't have
much of an appetite anymore. With no identification,
and no way of proving who she really was, she didn't
know how to get out of the mess she'd somehow found
herself in. Nobody seemed to want to believe that she
wasn't Rose Diamond.

She looked up at the cracked plaster ceiling, at the shadows dancing across it from the hallway lantern. "Why is this happening to me?" she whispered into the chilled air. "Why?"

"Because, madam, you simply couldn't leave well enough alone and be satisfied with the life you had."

Jane startled, and looked to her left through a blur of tears. There was a man standing outside her cell, glaring down his long, patrician nose at her. "I beg your pardon?" she said, sniffling.

"As well you should after *this* little fiasco. Do you have any idea what you've put me through trying to find you?"

Confused, Jane dashed at the moisture in her eyes and shook her head. "No, I . . . "

The man looked familiar, and she stared hard at him, trying to place where she might have seen him before. He was tall and slender, had thinning blond hair, and a deep cleft in his chin. His eyes were so small that in the meager light they looked like tiny hollows in his head.

She cautiously stood from the rickety cot beneath her. "Do . . . Do I know you?"

"Unfortunately, yes." Oddly enough, he walked determinedly forward and slammed right into the bars of her cell.

Jane blinked in astonishment.

And then, to her utter amazement, he glared at the bars, and then passed right through the solid wrought iron as if it weren't even there—strolled right into her cell without getting so much as a speck of dirt or grime on his impeccable white suit.

Jane took a startled step backward. "Good heavens! Who . . . ? *What* are you?"

"A very *irritable* and *put-upon* angel," he retorted. "Just *look* at you, Miss Baker. Your clothes are a disaster. Your hair is a fright. You look like a nuclear catastrophe!"

Jane's heart lurched. "You know me!" she cried excitedly. "You *know* that I'm *Jane Baker!*"

"All too well," he said blandly.

She rushed toward him. "Then you must be here to help me—to get me out of this mess."

He cocked his head and gave her an assessing look. "Miss Baker, are you at all aware of where you are?"

"I'm in jail. And for no good reason at all, I might add. These people think I'm a criminal," she added in a shocked whisper.

"Mmm hmm. But do you know *exactly* where you are?"

"Pine Oaks," she replied, wondering at his questions. Was he there to help her or not?

He rolled his eyes, apparently exasperated with her again. "Miss Baker, do you have any idea how you came to be here?"

The events of the past day flitted through Jane's mind—her fall from the rock wall, waking up in a field and being captured by Dolan Kincaid, riding for several uncomfortable hours on a horse, being in the middle of a deadly shoot-out, and then ending up behind bars. It had all been nothing short of a nightmare.

And now she was being visited by an irritable angel.

Suddenly her eyes flew open wide, and she gave the man in front of her a questioning look. To her horror, he nodded in acknowledgment. "My God," she rasped, tears filling her eyes again. "I'm in hell. I did die . . . when I fell, and—"

"No, no, you are *not* in hell. Good God, woman, pay attention! You are very much alive—and in a *great* deal of trouble!"

"What kind of trouble?"

"Just look *around* yourself! Haven't you noticed that you're not in *Kansas* anymore?"

"Of course I've noticed," she retorted; his tone was beginning to annoy her. "That blasted Mr. Kincaid snatched me right off my sidewalk and dragged me out into the wilderness—"

"He did not *snatch* you."

"Well, I certainly didn't go along willingly."

"You didn't go along at *all.* Mr. Kincaid found you in that meadow, just exactly as he claimed he did."

Jane blinked at him, and then broke into nervous laughter. "But that's ridiculous. How in the world did I end up out in the middle of nowhere, and with no memory of getting there? If I'm not dead, and Mr. Kincaid didn't kidnap me, then what, exactly, happened?"

The angel sighed. "What has happened to you is simple, Miss Baker. How to go about *solving* it is going to be the tricky part. In laymen's terms, you died from that ridiculous attempt to climb that wall this morning, and I, magnanimously, attempted to send you back to your body for a second chance. Things then proceeded to get all mucked up—you have *no* idea how temperamental computers can be—and you were returned to the wrong destination."

Jane stared at him with her mouth hanging open. His explanation didn't make any more sense to her than the situation itself. "Let me get this straight. You're an angel."

"Precisely."

"And I died this morning."

"Undeniably."

"And you tried to send me back, but messed up and sent me to the wrong place."

"Exact—" He broke into a frown.

"Mr. Angel—"

"Please," he interrupted holding up his hand, "call me Nelson. Mr. Angel makes me sound like a sponge cake."

"Nelson," she complied. "I don't see what all the fuss is about. Simply help me explain to these people who I really am, and then I'll catch the next bus back home."

"Bus?" He chuckled, shaking his head. "Miss Baker, a *bus,* as fine a mode of tranportation as it is, cannot return you home from here."

"But surely there's a town around here somewhere with a bus stop."

"Miss Baker, there *are* no buses," he said in exasperation. "No boats, no planes, no motor cars! Not a *single* luxury!"

Jane blanched at his outburst. "Then where, exactly, am I?"

He calmed himself by clearing his throat and tugging down on the hem of his white linen jacket. "You are *exactly* smack dab in the middle of the year 1890."

Now it was Jane's turn to laugh. "You're . . . you're joking."

But his expression was steadfastly serious. "I do not *joke.*"

Jane staggered backward and dropped down onto the cot behind her. "*1890*?" she rasped. "The *year* 1890?"

"That is correct."

"But that's . . . impossible!"

"That's precisely what skeptics said to Columbus when he claimed the world was round. It is also what people thought of landing on the moon at one point. And, if memory serves, what many said the day Miss Julia Roberts married Lyle Lovett. *Nothing* is impossible, Miss Baker."

"Then this town . . . these people . . . they're all . . . all . . ."

"*Tacky* is, I believe, the word you're searching for."

"They think I'm a criminal!"

"Yes. You seem to have arrived at a very fortuitous time for one Miss Rose Diamond."

"I saw her wanted poster!" Jane exclaimed. "The woman could be my *twin*!"

"The family resemblance is remarkable."

"Family resemblance?"

"Rose Diamond's actual name is Rosanna Baker, and she is your great-great-great-aunt. In 1890 she was considered to be one of the best cardsharps in the entire country. She was known for her sharp wit, icy heart, and firecracker temper. The woman was—*is*—a veritable Medusa."

Jane gaped. "I have an infamous outlaw for an ancestor?" The irony of the situation struck her, and she broke into laughter. "And these people think *I'm her*?"

"I'm glad you find this so amusing."

"Well, look at me, Nelson. Do I *look* like a Medusa?"

"You look like Rose Diamond, Miss Baker, dressed in a dirty shirt, and a stained skirt. That is all that matters to these people. It's not as if they can fingerprint you and verify your claims. Thus, we have a very serious problem on our hands."

Jane was still smiling. She couldn't get over the fact

that she was being mistaken for someone dire and dastardly. It was actually a little flattering.

". . . to get you back to 1997 before it's too late—
Miss Baker! Are you listening to me?! Rose Diamond is
hanged for her crimes in early June of 1890."

Jane frowned in sympathy. "That's very sad."

Nelson let out an impatient sigh. "Miss Baker, *you* are
Rose Diamond in the eyes of these people. And this is
June the second, 1890."

Realization finally dawned on Jane and she lurched to
her feet. "Well, send me back already!"

"That is my intention—"

"Now! Mr. Kincaid is determined to take me
Sacramento to stand trial. He said that I'd probably be
tried and hanged all in the same day!"

"All right, all right. But there is *one* . . . minor problem, Miss Baker."

"What?! What problem?!"

"I, um, I am not exactly sure *how* to get you back."

"*What!*" Jane was beginning to actually feel the sensation of a noose tightening around her neck. "How can the
angel who got me here not know how to get me back?!"

"I'm simply going to need some time to do some
research."

"What *kind* of research?"

"It shouldn't take long."

"*How* long?"

"Well, I'm not exactly sure."

She gave him a suspicious scowl. "You *can* get me
back. Can't you?"

One corner of Nelson's thin mouth twitched in an
expression that looked suspiciously like chagrin. "I'm
not exactly sure."

Jane clenched her fists, and fought a very strong impulse to scream. "You get me out of here this instant!" she shouted. "This very instant!"

"Now, now, Miss Baker. There is no need to panic."

"No need to panic? I'm being mistaken for a woman who's destined to die with a noose around her neck!"

"Just give me a few hours."

"What choice do I have? I certainly can't get back home on my own—I'm fresh out of ruby slippers!"

"Madam, believe me, more than just *your* fate hangs in the balance here—"

"Don't say *hangs*!" she blurted.

"Right. Sorry. Now . . . just stay put," he said with a firm gesture of his hands. "I don't want to have to go chasing all over the Old West looking for you again."

Jane made her own gesture, a futile one directed at the concrete block and iron walls surrounding her. "And where, exactly, would I go?"

He smiled weakly. "Yes, well, in the words of Arnold Schwarzenegger, I'll be back." With that, the angel faded into thin air.

Jane stared at the place where he'd been standing for quite some time before she finally looked away and sat back down on her cot. She'd longed for excitement, wished for something new in her life. Well, she supposed she'd just been given her life's quota in one giant dose.


No matter how hard he tried, Dolan couldn't seem to fall asleep.

He'd tossed and turned for an hour before finally getting up and heating himself a warm glass of milk. But even now, although he was lying on a soft, clean bed, with nothing but sturdy walls and blessed silence around, he was staring blindly at the beamed ceiling.

Rose Diamond was a witch. What other explanation could there be? Not only was she one hell of a poker player, she apparently had some sort of magical power over men that rendered them half-stupid—carried some kind of enchanted dust or something that she tossed at them when they weren't looking.

He was so tired his head was ringing, but thoughts of Rose Diamond and her long, sleek legs kept spinning through his head. Was she cold? Had he left her enough blankets? Was she hungry? Had she eaten the dinner she'd been given? Was she angry? Or was she still wearing that same doe-eyed expression she'd had when he'd slammed her cell door shut and left her lying there alone?

And the biggest question of all, the one nagging at Dolan unmercifully: Why the hell did he care?

What was it about Rose Diamond that had his stomach all tied up in knots?

Dolan knew one thing for sure: it would be considerably easier to resist the woman's charms if she'd only turn into the virago Jack had warned him about. Maybe in the morning he'd try badgering her into revealing her true self. If her temper was half what it was rumored to be, she had to be practically bursting at the seams from holding it in all day.

"Still awake?"

Dolan turned his attention to the doorway. Kristen was standing there, her rounded silhouette highlighted by the glow of the hall lamplight. She was smirking knowingly at him.

"I've got a lot on my mind," he replied moodily.

"And I bet she's got green eyes and blond hair." He shifted, hating her insight, and tucked his hands behind his head.

"Rose Diamond is only one of many things on my mind tonight."

"Uh huh. And another is a poker tournament with her name all over it. Face it, Dolan. In only one day that woman's managed to grab you by the nose hairs."

"It's nothing but a vague sexual attraction, Kristen. She's beautiful, and I'm only human."

"Vague?" she repeated with a short laugh. She leaned against the doorjamb. "Vague doesn't keep awake the only man I've ever seen fall asleep while perched in the saddle of a galloping horse."

Dolan was quiet for a moment. "She's not at all like what Jack described her to be."

"She's deceptive, Dolan. That's her strongest trait."

"When I left her in jail, she seemed . . . almost scared."

Kristen Ford broke into quiet laughter. "Scared? Rose Diamond? From what I hear, the only thing that could scare that woman is God Himself—and I wouldn't even bank on that. She's playing you, Dolan. Playing you like the family fiddle. And I suggest you get these romantic notions about her out of your head before they get you in trouble—or even killed."

Dolan snorted derisively. "Hell, there's nothing romantic going on here, Kristen."

"Be careful around her, Dolan. There's more to a woman like that than meets the eye."

He smiled at her, knowing she was seriously concerned for him. "You worry too much."

"Well, somebody's got to look out for you, Dolan Kincaid. *You* sure the hell don't." She smiled at him. "Good night," she said, turning from the door. "And if I don't see you in the morning before you leave, good luck."

Dolan redirected his gaze back to the ceiling. It was going to be one hell of a long night. And he had two more to go with an untouchable woman by his side whom he found sexy as hell.

Something pulled Jane out of a light sleep. She squinted up at the shadows being cast upon the ceiling by a lone lantern hanging outside her cell, and reminded herself of where she was. Hoping to find that it was Nelson who had awakened her, she sat up, but her cell was empty. Nelson still hadn't returned.

She caught the faint sound of muffled voices coming from the front office and listened carefully. Dare she hope that Dolan Kincaid had returned with the marshal? That they'd come to their senses and were letting her go?

When she heard the metallic jangling of keys coming down the hallway, she straightened and squinted into the darkness. A tall, gangly man broke through the shadows, followed by a short, squat man coming up behind him. Both men moved into the lantern light. Both were smiling broadly.

"We're sure awful sorry fer takin' so long," the short one said. "You . . . you all right? 'Cause we'd hate fer ya to be mad at us—"

The tall one gave him a sharp elbow in the ribs. "Would ya stop babblin' all over the place, Cleavus, and open the blasted door?" His high-pitched voice squeaked and cracked twice.

"Oh . . . oh, yeah. S-sure, Barn."

The short man produced a large set of keys and used them to open Jane's door. She stood, and watched them warily as they entered her cell. "What"—she cleared her throat—"what can I do for you gentlemen?"

"Gentlemen?" the short one said, with a frown creasing his high forehead. "Gosh, Barn," he whispered to his friend, "I think she *is* mad at us."

"'Course she's mad at us!" the skinny one retorted. "Took us a whole entire day to save her from that low-down bounty hunter! He didn't hurt ya, did he, Miss Rose?"

Jane shook her head jerkily and spotted the cloth bandage circling the upper arm of the shorter man. These had to be her two rescuers from earlier that day. Which meant they were friends of the dastardly Rose Diamond—which gave Jane ample reason to be wary of them.

"We done the best we could, Miss Rose. Cleavus, here, even took a bullet in the arm for ya. Show her, Cleavus," he snapped at his companion.

Cleavus held up his right arm and showed her the bloody bandage wrapped around his thick bicep.

"I'm . . . I'm sorry you were shot," Jane stammered. She wasn't sure how they'd react if she told them they'd risked their lives to save someone other than their friend, so she decided to keep the truth to herself.

Both men cocked their heads and gave her odd stares. Jane smiled hesitantly. It would be just her luck if *these* two happened to be the ones who finally figured out she wasn't Rose Diamond.

"Barn?" Cleavus whispered out of the side of his mouth. "Do you think she really meant that?"

"'Course not," Barney hissed back. "She thinks you're just as stupid as I do for gettin' shot." He smiled at Jane. "We gotta hurry, Miss Rose, before that deputy comes around."

Deputy Tuggle? He'd been so nice to her, bringing her dinner and extra blankets. "What did you do to him?" she asked, alarmed.

Barney sniffed proudly and rocked back on his heels. "We hit him with a board."

Jane's eyes rounded in horror. "A *board*?"

"A really thick one we found lyin' out by the trough," Cleavus added. "Although I still think a rock woulda done better. Like that round flat one I used to skip in the pond the other day. You know, Barn, the one as big around as my hand—well, not quite my hand—let me see your hand, Barn, and we can—"

Barney slapped Cleavus's hand away. "Would you knock it off! Miss Rose ain't interested in your skippin' rock. She just wants ta get outta this cold, damp cell!" He smiled at Jane again. "We really should be goin', Miss Rose."

Going? Nelson's warning rang through Jane's head, that she was to stay exactly where she was.

"Uh . . . um . . . go where?"

Both men gave her a blank stare, and then Barney snorted a laugh. "There she goes, testin' us again, Cleavus."

Cleavus broke into a grin and wagged a playful finger at her. "We're not gonna fall for that again. No sirree."

"We learned plenty the last time you got us to name our hideout in public, Miss Rose."

"I still got the lump to prove it," Cleavus grumbled, rubbing the back of his balding head.

Jane smiled and nodded—although she had no idea what they were talking about. "You want to take me to your hideout?"

"To *our* hideout," Barney clarified.

"Uhhh." Cleavus looked suddenly nervous. "Barn?" he whispered to his companion. "She always said it was *her* hideout and we was just guests."

"I know that!" Barney hissed. He smiled at Jane. "But *we* like to think of it as home. Now help the lady outside, Cleavus."

Cleavus stepped forward and held out his short, thick hand to her, and Jane stepped back and stared at it as if it belonged to the devil himself. How in the world did she explain to these two men that she didn't want to be rescued?

"Ummm . . . you know what?" She gave them what she hoped looked like a confident smile. "I think I'd rather stay here—just for tonight. I'm really"—she yawned for effect—"tired."

Cleavus lowered his outstretched hand, and frowned at her.

"No offense," Jane quickly added.

Barney considered her with beady, watery eyes. Knowing Rose as well as they obviously did, they had to suspect that something wasn't quite right. Jane continued to smile at them, though, hoping she could at least keep them calm.

Finally Barney sniffed and crossed his thin arms over his bony chest. "She's obviously in shock, Cleavus. I guess we're left with only one choice."

"Choice?" Jane repeated.

"You want I should?" Cleavus asked him.

Barney nodded. "Yup. Pick her up."

Jane gasped as the stocky man stepped forward and hefted her up in the air. She slammed down hard over his beefy shoulder, and all the breath was pushed out of her lungs—preventing her from letting out the bloodcurdling scream that was her first impulse.

The floor spun, dizzyingly, beneath her as she was carted out of her cell and down the hallway. "Stop!" she managed to croak. "Wait!"

But her rasped protests were either not heard or totally ignored.

She was carried through the front office, where poor Deputy Tuggle was sprawled, unconscious, on the floor. The front door was thrown open, and the moonlight illuminated the planks of the boardwalk, and then the packed dirt of the road, as she was hauled out into the street like an oversized sack of potatoes.

"Put her up on her horse, Cleavus," Barney ordered in a whisper.

*No!* Jane's mind screamed. *Anything but another horse!*

"Are you sure she's not gonna hurt me when I let her go?"

"I'll hurt ya worse if ya don't do as I say! Now, get her up on that horse!"

The next thing Jane knew she was right back in the saddle again; the one place she'd hoped to avoid for the rest of her natural life. Every muscle in her lower body screamed in protest, and she immediately began to dismount. It was time to set niceties aside, and get down to brass tacks. "Gentlemen, thank you, but I do *not* want to be rescued—"

"Miss Rose," Barney quickly interjected, causing Jane to freeze, perched in the stirrup. "If you get off that horse, well . . . we'll be forced to tie you to it."

Jane gave him a startled glare. "Well, that would certainly be an interesting way to *rescue* someone," she retorted.

"Ah, Miss Rose, we know you're just testin' us." He nudged Cleavus and they both laughed at what they apparently thought was a great big joke. "And we aim to pass this time."

"Look, gentlemen. I have had a *very* long day, and I would really appreciate returning to my cell for a little more sleep. Why don't you come back in the morning?" she offered with another feigned smile. By then Nelson would have returned and this whole nightmare would be over.

Barney's and Cleavus's laughter intensified. "I always said she was a downright amusin' woman," Cleavus chortled.

"A regular comedian." Barney grinned in admiration. "Now you get back on up there, Miss Rose, before we have ta tie ya up for your own good."

"*For my own good?*"

"And you best keep your voice down. I know how much you hate gunfights, but there's bound to be one if this town gets woken up."

The very last thing Jane wanted to be responsible for was a gunfight, but she wasn't about to leave and ruin Nelson's chances of finding her. She dropped down to the ground, and turned to face her two "rescuers."

"Thank you, gentlemen, for your effort. But I choose not to be saved."

With that, she brushed past them for the jailhouse.

"Grab her, Cleavus!"

Jane was caught from behind by a pair of thick, strong arms that lifted her clear off the ground. She kicked her feet and opened her mouth to let out an ear-piercing scream, but a stale rag was stuffed down her throat, preventing her from making more than a muffled attempt.

Without preamble, she was tossed back onto her horse, where her hands were tied securely to the pommel of her saddle. Barney and Cleavus then mounted their horses, and led her unceremoniously out of town.

From death, to a bounty hunter, to jail, to the company of two outlaws, Jane somehow kept managing to jump out of one damn frying pan right into the next.

# 7

*Three horrible hours later,* the morning sun finally began to rise, bright and hot, over the tree-lined hillsides. It glared down through the dense branches and foliage and straight into Jane's eyes. It heated her already sunburned nose, reminded her of how dry her mouth was, and basically added to her already elevated irritability.

Once they'd ridden far enough from Pine Oaks, to prevent her from finding her way back in the dark, Cleavus and Barney had taken the gag out of her mouth and untied her hands. They'd shared some hard biscuits and dried beef with her—which was certainly more than Jane could say about her previous abductor, but at least with Dolan Kincaid she'd been sustained by the impression, no matter how misguided, that she'd be rescued at any moment. In contrast, however, now she knew that each step taken away from Pine Oaks made it harder and harder for Nelson to find her.

Barney and Cleavus had tried engaging her in polite conversation, but Jane simply wasn't in the mood to play nice. Her body had gone from sore to numb, her thoughts from dismal to morose, and her usual optimism was ebbing at an all-time low. She was being pushed way beyond her level of tolerance.

"I don't know," she heard Cleavus saying to Barney. The two men were riding a few yards ahead of her. "She just *seems* different."

"You been eatin' strange roots again, Cleavus?" Barney retorted. "Next thing I know you're gonna be dancin' naked with another skunk on your head."

"I ain't eaten a root in over six days—and that skunk was as tame as molasses." Cleavus stole a quick glance back at Jane, who instantly took a keen interest in the passing vegetation. "I'm tellin' ya, she's *different*."

"Well, at least gimme a fer instance, here, Cleavus."

"All right. She hasn't hollered at us once. How 'bout that? Not one holler this whole entire time."

"*Maybe* she's just satisfied with our handlin' of this whole unfortunate situation?"

"And since when have you known Miss Rose to be satisfied with anything?"

There was a moment of silence, and then Barney turned in his saddle and gave Jane a quick backward glance—this time Jane busied herself with brushing something from her filthy skirt. "Maybe she's just tired," Barney hissed back. "And hungry. You saw the way she wolfed down that biscuit and jerked beef."

"Saw it? I was afraid to get my hands too close. Hey, maybe she's sick."

"Don't say that! She'd skin us alive if we left her in Kincaid's hands long enough to get sick! No, no, she's healthy as a horse."

Jane had been listening to their varied conversations

all morning, most of which had something to do with her—or rather Rose Diamond. The two men seemed to put a lot of stock into what Rose Diamond thought and felt. In fact, it was pretty clear to Jane that the two men were more than a little afraid of the woman.

"Do ya . . . do ya think she'll make us sleep outside tonight?"

"If she does you're gonna be a man about it for once, Cleavus."

"Aw, Barn," Cleavus whined, "you know how I feel about wolves."

"Which would you rather face, wolves or Miss Rose?" It took a moment, but Cleavus finally grumbled, "Wolves."

*Correction,* Jane thought to herself. They weren't simply afraid of Rose Diamond, they were *terrified* of her. Regardless of whatever crime her Aunt Rosanna had committed, Jane couldn't help but admire a woman who demanded so much respect. It was the one thing Jane had longed for all her life, and had failed miserably in acquiring.

A tight cramp suddenly dug into her left calf and she let out a painful gasp. Holding tightly to the pommel with her right hand, she leaned to one side and tried to massage the pain loose. She didn't know how much more of this she could take. How long were these fools going to ride before stopping for a blasted rest? Did she have to fall over dead before they finally relented?

"Damn," she hissed, rubbing her calf with all her might.

Barney turned and gave her an alarmed look. "You all right, Miss Rose?"

"No, I am not all right," she snapped.

Cleavus turned and joined Barney in looking apprehensively at her. And that was when realization finally dawned on Jane. Yes, these men were afraid of Rose Diamond. And, at the moment, they thought *she* was Rose.

After all Jane had put up with in the past twenty-four hours because of her uncanny resemblance to her notorious relative, it was high time that resemblance worked a little in her favor. She took a deep breath—to bolster her courage, and cleared her throat loudly. "Hey, you guys!" she bellowed in what she imagined to be her best Rosanna Baker voice.

Both men swung toward her so fast, they just about fell off their horses. "Yes, Miss Rose?" Barney squeaked.

Jane narrowed her eyes on him. "Do you two intend to ride me to my death?" she demanded. "How much farther?"

"Ah . . . ha . . . ta . . . 'bout two hours," Cleavus finally got out.

"Well, I'm gettin' tired!" she barked.

"Uh, s-sorry, Miss Rose," Cleavus stammered. "M-maybe we should move a little faster—"

Barney gave Cleavus a smack on the back of the head. "You don't move faster when a lady's gettin' tired, you idiot!" He turned a bright smile on Jane. "Would you like to stop and rest, Miss Rose?"

Jane's first impulse was to smile out of sheer relief, but she kept up her act and gave Barney a cold, hard stare. "What do *you* think?"

"I . . . ta . . . I think maybe . . . yes?" he answered.

"Then why haven't we stopped?!" she demanded. The two men immediately brought their horses to a halt and practically killed themselves leaping to the ground.

"Not here," Jane said, disdainfully turning up her nose. "There's too much shade."

Without missing a beat, the two men bounded right back into their saddles, and Jane smiled in satisfaction. Power was definitely heady. "Where would *you* like to stop, Miss Rose?" Barney asked sweetly.

Enjoying herself immensely, Jane made a show of glancing around the tree-lined trail. Then she looked up ahead where the beginnings of a large clearing could be seen. "Up there will do nicely."

"Well, up there sounds just wonderful ta us," Cleavus replied.

The two men led her—quickly—to the clearing. But once there, an argument ensued over who was *not* going to have to help "Rose" down off her horse.

"I carried her out of the jail," Cleavus insisted.

"That's 'cause yer bigger than me," Barney argued. "Look at me. I'm a puny little thing. Liftin' her's likely ta break my brittle spine."

"That's better'n her doin' it on purpose," Cleavus grumbled.

Jane wasn't going to sit in that hard saddle one second longer than she had to, however, and solved their problem by dismounting on her own. Her legs were tingling and wobbly, and she immediately sank to the ground. Barney and Cleavus both let out cries of alarm and hurried toward her. She waved them off, though, too tired to settle an argument over who was going to have to help her to her feet. Besides, she thought, lying down and stretching out in the grass and wildflowers, she could use a little relaxation, maybe even a little nap.

She closed her eyes, and smiled at how good it felt to take charge for once. Although she was pretending to be

someone else, her show of courage had actually bolstered her self-confidence a bit. She felt stronger than
she'd felt in years.

A few silent minutes passed with nothing but the
wind in the trees and the birds overhead to remind her
of where she was. Then she heard the restless shuffle of
Barney's and Cleavus's feet. "Do ya think she fell
asleep?"

"Shoot, Cleavus, how the dickens am I supposed ta
know?"

More peaceful silence. And then, "Well, are we just
gonna let her lie there?"

"Tell you what," Barney snapped. "How 'bout you go
on over there and wake her up?"

"Not me."

"Then I guess we're just gonna let her lie there, ain't
we!"

Jane smiled to herself. She wasn't leaving that
meadow until she was damn good and ready.

And then a loud shout came from the woods behind
her. "Barney! Cleavus! I have had about all I'm gonna
take from you two!"

Jane immediately recognized that deep, gritty—
angry—voice, and bolted upright in the grass just in time
to see Barney and Cleavus make a mad, clamoring dash
for cover toward the opposite side of the clearing.

"Yeah, you better run!" came another shout from the
trees. "I'm gonna skin you two alive!"

"Good lord, when will it all end?" Jane whispered to the
sky. She climbed to her feet on wobbly legs, and faced in
the direction the shouting was coming from. "Mr. Kincaid,"
she began, "threats are completely uncalled for—"

Two shots rang out from the trees where Cleavus and

Barney had hidden, and Jane turned toward the pair with a startled look. Dolan Kincaid fired back, and Jane went diving back down into the tall grass, where she covered her head and began screaming for Nelson. Where was that damn angel anyway?!

The bullets were whizzing over her head like crazed bumblebees, and she managed to crawl to cover behind a large boulder a few feet away. "You people are crazy!" she shouted above the clamor. A bullet zinged off the rock close to her head. "Stop firing at *me!*"

Black, acrid smoke was beginning to fill the clearing, a result of all the shooting, and Jane figured the blasted men would probably go on like this until they either killed each other or ran out of bullets. She turned and leaned back against the boulder to wait it out.

"Miss Baker, what in God's name are you doing *here?* I expressly told you to stay put!"

Jane quickly turned and found her disgruntled angel sitting on the top of the boulder. He seemed completely oblivious to the racket going on around him. "Nelson!" she cried. "Get me out of here!"

"Why couldn't you simply wait in that cell until my return? Young lady, you are going to be the end of me yet!"

"Well, forgive me," she shouted above the noise, "but when two men decide to bodily carry me away, there's not a whole lot I can do about it!"

"Certainly you could have—" He frowned as a barrage of rapidly fired shots drowned out his voice. He finally took a good look around the clearing. "*What* in heaven's name is going on here?"

"These men are trying to *kill* each other," Jane retorted. "And they don't seem to care whether or not *I* get killed in the process!"

"Ridiculous," Nelson muttered. "It's a wonder this country ever made it into the twentieth century. How are you holding up, Miss— Oooh, not so good, I see."

Jane was glaring ferociously at him. "*Get me out of here*," she demanded. "If I have to sit in one more saddle, or dodge one more bullet, I am seriously going to injure someone!"

Nelson gave her a hesitant smile. "Oh now, it can't be all that bad—"

"Not that bad?!" Jane blustered. "I have blisters on top of blisters, my legs are *permanently* bowed, and if one more gnat flutters up my nose I am going to lose what little breakfast I had this morning!"

"I see," Nelson said curtly. "Well . . . we have a minor problem."

Jane narrowed her eyes. "What kind of minor problem?"

"It seems that returning you to the twentieth century won't be as easy as I first imagined."

"But, considering you've had all night, I'm sure you've worked all the nasty little kinks out of the process," Jane said carefully.

"I wouldn't exactly say that."

Another bullet zinged off the boulder, and Jane ducked as the metallic sound chimed loudly in her ears. "Is that 'yes,' you've worked out the kinks, or 'no,' you've failed miserably?" she demanded.

"Young lady, I am doing the *best* that I can. Do you think it's *easy* watching over the flock of the world? You people are always getting into one *ridiculous* scrape after another—skiing into avalanches, bungee-jumping off bridges, *falling from rock walls*," he added with a pointed glare.

"Stop hedging, Nelson, and tell me what you know!" Jane shouted above the noise. For crying out loud, how many bullets could three men possibly carry?

Nelson glanced casually over his shoulder at the melee. "The, um, the only way I can see to send you home is for you to . . . well . . . to die again."

"*What?!*"

"Oh, it's very simple, Miss Baker," he snipped. "Simply stand up and take a bullet!"

Jane's mouth dropped wide open. "What kind of guardian angel are you?!" she demanded.

"Well, you don't have to act as though it were the most horrible thing in the world," Nelson replied defensively. "It's not as if you haven't done it before."

"*Unintentionally! I died unintentionally!*"

"Then think of it this way, Miss Baker." He gave her a snide smile. "Practice makes perfect."

Jane gritted her teeth. Was it possible to strangle a heavenly being? "You, sir, are out of your angelic mind!"

"Oh, come now, it won't be that bad. It will all be over very quickly—"

"Or very slowly and painfully if I'm unlucky enough to get shot by Barney or Cleavus! I could linger for days! Just . . . just give me a heart attack or something."

"Miss Baker, *I* am an angel. *We do not give heart attacks.*"

"Some angel. *What in God's name am I supposed to do now?*"

In that instant all the shooting finally stopped, and Jane's loud shout rang, strong and clear, through the silent meadow.

"I can answer that," Dolan Kincaid replied, stepping

out from a cluster of trees to her left. He strode toward
her with both their horses in tow. His square jaw was
tight, and his blue eyes were glittering like cold steel as
he stopped directly in front of her. "You can mount the
hell up."

Jane groaned and sank back against the boulder
behind her. "Dear God, anything," she whispered, "*anything* but that."

Dolan had never been so furious in his life. Here he'd
slept like hell the night before because of his perplexing
lady prisoner—he still didn't know what the hell was
wrong with him, but it was getting damned annoying, to
say the least. The woman was a criminal, for Christ's
sake. But every time she looked at him with those wide
green eyes of hers he suddenly found it hard to breathe.
There was just something about her, something that
didn't quite add up to him.

Hell, he'd actually been anxious to see her again that
morning. And he'd been hotter than hell when he'd
stepped into the jailhouse and found her gone.

Deputy Tuggle, though still dazed by a blow to the
back of his head, identified Rose's accomplices as
Barney Rollins and Cleavus Coltrain, and the two men
went from being a thorn in Dolan's side to an all-out
brier patch in his path. He'd had all he was going to take
from them.

His intent, when he found the pair, was to drag them
back to Pine Oaks, where they'd be kept in jail and out
of his way for the next few days. But, after a wild shoot-
out, in which they'd done nothing but ventilate foliage,
Barney and Cleavus had run off again before Dolan

could get his hands on either one of them. And he wasn't about to go chasing after them and take the chance of losing Rose again.

As for the lady herself, she had absolutely refused to mount up on her own. And so Dolan had been forced to pick her up and put her bodily on her horse once again.

The woman just didn't know when to quit. She was still insisting that she wasn't Rose Diamond, that she knew nothing about the charges against her. And now, the capper to Dolan's glorious morning, she wouldn't shut the hell up.

"You have got to be joking," she stated loud and clear. "That has got to be the *worst* idea I have ever heard."

Dolan would have gladly answered her—if she'd been talking to him. No, Rose Diamond was riding along behind him, staring into thin air, and having a lovely conversation with herself. And she seemed to be working up a good head of steam in the process.

"Oh, there's another brilliant suggestion," she snapped. Before Dolan had left that morning, Jack had warned him one more time that Rose wouldn't be an easy companion to deal with for the next two days. And, at this point in time, Dolan didn't think he'd ever been faced with such a glaring understatement.

"No! Absolutely *not!*" she shouted. "Something like that could maim me for life!"

Christ, if she didn't stop that incessant babbling, *he* was going to maim her for life.

"Do you have any idea how much that could hurt?" she added. "No, I will *not* keep my voice down—I don't care if he can hear me. The man already thinks I'm a criminal; adding insanity to the mix certainly won't make a difference."

There was a moment of silence, as if she were listening to a reply, and then, "You know, Nelson, it sounds suspiciously as if you are determined to blame this entire situation on me, when it was you who landed me here in the first place." Pause. "Well, then I suggest you stop wasting time, and flutter off and find a solution to this mess!"

Dolan looked back again, almost expecting to see something flitting off into the sky, and met Rose Diamond eye to eye. She gave him a bright smile, one so impacting it made him flinch. "Nice day, isn't it?" she said.

"Are you talking to *me* now?"

"Of course I am."

"Then I can assume you're finished with this little charade?"

A frown settled over her sunburned complexion. "Guides can only be seen by their clients."

"Guides?"

"Spiritual guides. Nelson prefers that title over angel."

"You've been talking to an angel," Dolan said flatly.

"He's trying to get me back home. Unfortunately he's running into a few snags."

"Right." Dolan turned his attention back to the tree-lined path, wondering what the hell the woman would come up with to aggravate him next. He had to admit, she had a quick mind on her. And an unsurpassable acting talent.

The grass and dirt trail widened a few moments later, and he glanced over to find her urging her horse up next to his. At her earlier pleading, he'd relented and let her guide her own mount along behind him—something he was certain he was going to regret eventually.

"I want you to know, Mr. Kincaid," she said, "that I understand why you've been so rude to me since our meeting yesterday."

"Really," he replied flatly.

"You don't trust me. And, considering who you think I am, that's very reasonable."

He gave her a sidelong glance. The sun was glinting off her dark gold hair, and reflecting in her deep, green eyes. "Your understanding means the world to me," he remarked.

"And I'm going to try my best not to take your mistrust of me personally."

"I suppose there's something to be said for ignorant bliss." He ducked to avoid a low-hanging branch as they headed up a slight incline. A white-tailed deer scampered across their path, and he watched it until it disappeared into the dense trees.

"Do you believe in life after death, Mr. Kincaid?"

He smirked. "Hoping for another chance, Miss Diamond?"

"I would appreciate it if you would please stop calling me that."

"And what would you like me to call you?"

"*Jane* would be nice."

He grunted and glanced over at her. As usual, she was clinging to her saddle horn as if her very life depended on it. "And if I don't call you Jane?"

"Then, Mr. Kincaid, you will probably find yourself ignored."

Unlike yesterday, Dolan's lady prisoner was sporting

quite an attitude this morning. Even further proof, as far as he was concerned, that she was holding back her true colors.

"So then, is this what you do for a living?" she asked. "Hunt criminals?"

He nodded. "Yep."

"It sounds dangerous."

"And being a cardsharp is akin to knitting stockings?"

"I wouldn't know. *I* am a librarian."

He shook his head at her determination to cling to her ridiculous story—even after Jack had identified her as Rose Diamond. If he intended to get anywhere with her, he had to make her admit to the truth. "Tell me something. Do you like moving from town to town, game to game, or do you long for that one big tournament that would set you up for life?"

"Mr. Kincaid, the only cards I deal with have the names of books and authors on them."

Dolan rolled his eyes heavenward; the woman wasn't only sharp, she was stubborn to the core. "When are you going to let up on this tired story, Miss Diamond?"

"When are you going to listen to reason, Mr. Kincaid?"

"Oh"—he laughed coldly—"I think I've been pretty damn reasonable, lady."

"Maybe to a criminal, but *I* am not a criminal."

He sighed; he had only three days 'til the tournament —three days to bring her around to his way of thinking, and an argument was going to get him absolutely nowhere. "We've chased this tail around and around, Miss Dia—"

"One would think that you didn't want me to be anyone *but* Rose Diamond."

Now that hit just a little too close to home. It was true that if she were anyone other than Rose he'd be kissing that poker tourney good-bye for another full year.

She let out an impatient groan. "Why am I even bothering to talk to you?"

"Because your invisible angel left?"

"*Guide,*" she retorted. "Nelson is a *spiritual guide.*"

"Right."

There was a tense pause in their conversation as they crossed a shallow, rocky creek side by side. She certainly seemed determined to convince him she was an unassuming librarian. But then he'd probably do the same if it was his neck headed for a noose.

"So," she said, when they were back on dry ground, "what, exactly, did Rose do to merit your hearty pursuit?"

"You're wanted in four states for robbery and horse thieving."

"*Four?*"

"But you really topped yourself in Sacramento last month." He gave her a considering look. "Murder is something you've never dabbled in before. Which makes me wonder if you were aware you'd killed that man when you left him bleeding in that dark alley?"

"I . . . Well . . ." she stammered, "what was he doing with Rose in a dark alley in the first place?"

"Story is, he was wildly attracted to you. And you encouraged him to follow you outside. You tried to rob him and he resisted."

"Well maybe *he* attacked *her*, Mr. Kincaid, and . . . and she was forced to defend herself."

"Death is a pretty high price to pay for a few stolen kisses."

"Maybe he was trying to steal more than a few kisses," she replied indignantly.

He turned and narrowed his eyes on her. "What are you saying? That he attacked you?"

"How should *I* know?" she exclaimed. "*I* wasn't there, *Rose* was!"

Dolan clenched his jaw. "Is that the story you intend to tell the judge, Miss Diamond? That you couldn't possibly have shot the man because you weren't even there? Because you aren't Rose Diamond? I assure you, the district attorney will produce twenty people who will swear to exactly who you are."

"I don't intend to tell anything to a judge, Mr. Kincaid, because by that time I intend to be long gone. Nelson will have come up with a solution for sending me home by then."

Dolan broke into sardonic chuckles. "So you're going to rely on heavenly intervention?"

"And now you're going to tell me that you don't believe in heaven?"

"Oh, I believe in heaven. I just don't happen to believe that angels are in the business of helping criminals like yourself escape justice."

"Justice has nothing to do with this, Mr. Kincaid. I am here by mistake. Nelson is attempting to correct things."

"Things?"

"He's doing his best to return me to the twentieth century, where I belong."

"*Return* you?" he repeated incredulously.

"That's where I'm from. The year 1997. I'm a librarian in the small town of Littleville, California. I live at 2785 Maple Lane. My phone number is 241-7985. I was born in San Francisco on June 2, 1967. And you, Mr. Kincaid, are roughly one hundred years older than I am." She gave him a tight smile. "You wear it well."

That was the last straw. Dolan had absolutely had it with her asinine stories. He brought his horse to a neck-wrenching halt, stopping hers in its tracks in the process. "That's it," he growled. He pointed a rigid finger at her. "One more word out of you about angels or the twentieth century and I'm gonna tie your jaw closed, do you understand me?!"

She blinked at his shout, and nodded mutely.

"And another thing," he added. "Those timid, innocent stares? Knock 'em the *hell* off! They're really beginning to chap my ass!"

That said, he whirled his horse around and headed back down the trail ahead of her, feeling frustrated and furious. She was spouting out fairy tales as if she were the Brothers Grimm, for God's sake, and he wasn't about to listen to another word of it.

"There's no need to turn belligerent," she grumbled from behind him a few moments later.

"If you've got something to say, lady, then speak the hell up." He was starting to feel guilty for shouting at her, which only made him more angry—at *himself.* Christ, the woman was tying him up in knots.

"I said," she replied more forcefully, "that there is no need for you to become belligerent. Why are you so angry anyway? I would think you'd be feeling much better after a comfortable night's sleep."

Dolan gritted his teeth. Why was he so angry? Because she was driving him completely nuts!

"I hope this doesn't have anything to do with me leaving the jail with Barney and Cleavus."

He turned sharply toward her. "Let's talk about that, shall we, Miss Diamond? Did you *honestly* believe you'd get away with two men who couldn't rescue a thought from their own damn brains?"

"I had no choice but to go with them."

He laughed at that absurd reply. "Women like Rose Diamond make their own choices."

She sighed with dramatic exasperation. "That is my point, Mr. Kincaid. We are not talking about Rose Diamond. *I* am—"

He threw her a sharp look of warning, and she immediately clamped her lips shut. "Save it for the judge, Miss Diamond. Maybe you'll get lucky and he won't be as *belligerent* as I am. Although, considering it was his brother you killed, I wouldn't count on that."

She let out a sharp gasp and Dolan glanced over to see her looking pale. "I'd say *that's* a conflict of interest," she replied.

He shrugged, liking this little twist he'd added to her situation—the truth was, she'd shot some ne'er-do-well who'd ended up buried on boot hill. She wasn't the only one who could make up a good story. "I don't think Hanging Judge Colfax is going to care."

"*Hanging* Judge Colfax?" she repeated hoarsely.

"Ninety percent of his convictions end up getting their necks stretched."

"Well . . . well, I have nothing to worry about. I am *not* Rose Diamond."

"You just keep saying that, lady," Dolan replied with a wry twist of his lips. He had her right where he wanted her. "And I'll be sure they etch it into your tombstone."

# 8

*The day wore on for Jane* as she was led across lush plateaus and through densely treed forests. Dolan Kincaid said very little to her, and she stubbornly told herself that it didn't matter whether he believed who she was or not. She wouldn't be around long enough to face "Hanging Judge Colfax," thus she simply wouldn't hang. Still, it rankled that Dolan Kincaid continued to think so little of her.

The sun was beginning to set—and her stomach was becoming painfully empty—when he finally reined in beside a wide stream and announced that they'd be making camp for the night. Jane was relieved on one hand, but disappointed on the other: She'd been hoping that Nelson would have come through for her by now, that she'd be resting comfortably at home in her easy chair.

"Climb down."

She flashed Dolan Kincaid an irritated look. He'd already dismounted and was waiting for her to do the same. "Just once I'd like to hear you use the word 'please,' Mr. Kincaid." She suspected hell would freeze over first.

"And just once I'd like you to do as you're told without giving me any trouble."

Trouble? Agreeing to get out of the saddle was certainly no trouble at all for Jane. However the actual *act* of doing so was bound to give her problems.

She gritted her teeth and carefully leaned forward, slowly taking the weight and pressure off her abused backside. Groaning at the ache in her thighs, she slowly, carefully, edged her right foot up and over the back of her horse. Then she paused, poised rigidly in the stirrup, before oh so gently lowering herself to the ground. Once she was on her feet, her legs wavered like two disjointed twigs, forcing her to lean against her smelly horse for support. Her smelly horse didn't like the intrusion and sidestepped away from her, almost sending Jane in a nosedive to the ground.

"You've got five minutes to unsaddle that animal and get your bedroll set up by that thick pine over there."

Jane sent Dolan a glare that rivaled the fires of hell. She was sore, hungry, sick to death of his bossiness— and she was just too damn exhausted to be afraid of him. "Or what?" she demanded. "You'll shoot me? Well, I've got news for you, Mr. Kincaid; at this point I'd *welcome* the deliverance."

His fingers paused over the large buckle on his saddle cinch as he glanced over at her, his tall, lean profile silhouetted by the setting sun behind him. "Or you won't eat," he said simply.

Jane gasped; he certainly knew how to hit a girl where she lived. She stood there in frustrated silence, getting her bearings as he finished with the cinch and hefted his saddle off his horse. She watched the muscles in his arms bulge against the seams of his blue cotton shirt. He was a powerful, not to mention attractive, man, and she found herself unable to keep from staring at him in the waning daylight.

*"What?"*

His sharp question pulled her out of her mesmerized daze. She cleared her throat, realizing she'd been caught blatantly staring at him, and made a show of brushing off her skirt. "Nothing."

"I suggest you get moving, Miss Diamond." He set his saddle down. "Or you'll be sleeping on the cold, bare ground tonight with an empty stomach."

Jane turned toward her horse and began tugging at the leather thongs holding the thin bedroll to the back of her saddle. She suddenly felt very self-conscious, and hoped he wasn't watching her. "I, um, I'm assuming we'll be having a *large* dinner?"

"Hungry?"

"Starved."

"Good. Then you won't mind building a fire."

She gave him a baleful look. "I don't know the first thing about building a campfire, Mr. Kincaid. The next thing I know you'll be expecting me to go hunt down my own meal."

"Naw. It's difficult to track baked beans and biscuits in the dark."

Rolling her eyes, she carried her bedroll to the thick tree he'd indicated, kicked aside a few pinecones and rocks, and unrolled the tarp and blankets on the ground.

"You know, you probably wouldn't be so hungry if you'd stuck around the jail long enough to get breakfast." He shook his own bedroll open, and laid it on the ground a few feet from hers.

"Which I would have gladly done, Mr. Kincaid, if Barney and Cleavus hadn't insisted otherwise."

"Oh, that's right. It was *their* fault."

She gave him a steady glare. "That's right, Mr. Kincaid, it was."

He stared at her through his eyelashes. "See to your horse."

Exasperated, not to mention tired, Jane followed his command and walked back to her horse. She wavered, however, when she came face-to-face with the task of removing the animal's saddle. The leather contraption looked heavy—very, very heavy.

But she was determined to be just as proficient at the task as Dolan Kincaid had been a few minutes before. She began unbuckling the cinch strap, and the saddle immediately began sliding toward her on its thick wool blanket. Jane quickly braced her feet against the ground and moved to hold it in place on her horse's back, but, in the end, she only gave the thing something soft to land on. She ended up on her back, with the heavy saddle lying across her hips, pinning her to the ground.

"Interesting technique," Dolan Kincaid remarked, standing over her. He lifted the saddle off her with one hand, and dropped it on the ground beside his. "Go sit on your bedroll," he ordered impatiently.

Though the sore muscles in her legs rebelled, Jane managed to struggle to her feet. "Mr. Kincaid, I am doing the best I can under the circumstances, and I would appreciate a little more understanding!"

He crossed his arms over his broad chest. "And what circumstances would those be, Miss Diamond?"

She sighed. "I have asked you repeatedly, politely, *not* to call me that."

He gave her a look that said he couldn't have cared less what she'd asked of him.

"I have never unsaddled a horse before," she stated succinctly. She threw out her arms. "I have never done *any* of this before!"

"Now *that*," he replied, "is something I can finally believe. Go sit down."

His disgust with her was fully apparent. Jane stomped over to her bedroll, and dropped down onto the ground. She fell back against the tree trunk, and pulled her legs up to her chest beneath her dirty skirt. For two solid days she'd wanted this man to believe something—anything—she said. However, having faith in her incompetence wasn't exactly what she'd had in mind.

The sun was dropping fast, raising a slight chill in the air, and she glanced around at the inhospitable, raw wilderness surrounding her. The forest was bound to be pitch black in a few minutes, and she wondered what kinds of animals were lurking out there just beyond the tree line. The idea of being shrouded in darkness until morning made her sore muscles tighten.

"Hold out your hands."

She looked up to find Dolan Kincaid looming over her with a long length of rope. She frowned at him. "What's that for?"

"I'm not gonna take any chances on you running away from me again. Now hold out your hands," he repeated, crouching down beside her.

Jane's heart nearly stopped. He intended to tie her up? In minutes she'd be sitting in pitch blackness, surrounded by miles and miles of wilderness—not to mention various kinds of ravenous wild animals—and he was going to tie her up? The man might as well ring the damn dinner bell!

"Mr. Kincaid," she said frantically, leaning away from him *and* his intentions, "I promise you, I will not run away."

"Your right hand, Miss Diamond," he persisted.

She stared at his intense face, her mind whirling as she tried to come up with something to say—anything that might change his mind.

Finally he reached out and took hold of her right hand himself. He began wrapping the rough hemp around her wrist, and Jane panicked. "Mr. Kincaid!" she exclaimed, struggling to break free of his iron grip, "this is *totally* unnecessary!"

"Hold still, goddamn it, or I'll truss you up face first on the ground."

Knowing he would do just that, and knowing it would place her in an even more precarious situation, Jane somehow managed to calm herself. "Listen, I . . . I understand why you would be so mistrusting of me, but—" She gasped as he reached for her other wrist and began tying the two together.

"No buts. You can't be trusted."

"Mr. Kincaid, this is *outrageous!* I'm not going to run off out here in the middle of nowhere!"

"Rose Diamond would do anything to keep from going to jail."

"I am *not* Rose Diamond. I am *Jane Baker! Jane Baker!*" And Jane Baker certainly didn't have the courage to race off into the wilderness in the dead of night!

He finished with her wrists, and picked up another long piece of rope lying at his feet. "You'll forgive me if I don't take your word for it." Wordlessly, he began wrapping the next length of thick rope around her stomach and the tree.

Jane closed her eyes, unable to stop tears from forming. She held herself rigid as he finished his task, while praying for her sanity through the coming night. When he was through, she opened her damp eyes and gazed into his. "I wouldn't run away," she whispered, her chin trembling. "I wouldn't."

All at once his expression softened, the hard creases around his mouth melting into faint character lines. He reached out and brushed away one of her tears as it dropped from her lashes and slipped down her face. "I'm sorry this has to be necessary." His hand lingered long enough to brush his fingers over her cheek and down along her jaw.

"Please," she begged. "Please don't do this."

As if her plea had burned him, he quickly rose to his feet and dragged both of his hands through his hair. Then he broke into faint laughter. "Are you this good at manipulating everybody, or am I just the lucky sucker?"

She shook her head, not understanding.

He laughed at himself again, and then turned away from her, heading toward the woods.

"Where are you going?" she cried.

"To get some firewood. Feel free to wait here." As he disappeared into the thick growth of trees and the mounting darkness, Jane fought the urge to scream, afraid that if she started she'd never be able to stop. Her hands were bound so tightly she doubted she'd be able to move them after they were freed.

She was only a librarian from the tiny town of Littleville, for crying out loud—not Calamity Jane!

Seconds ticked by, which turned into long, lingering

minutes as she waited for Dolan Kincaid to return. Finally, as the last glimmers of light began to fade from the sky, she could stand the tension no longer.

"*Nelsooooon!*" she shouted into the cool night air. "*Get . . . me . . . out of here!*"

"Saw some feathers over in the woods there," Dolan Kincaid replied as he strode back into their campsite with a load of small logs and tangled branches in his arms. "Maybe the wolves ate your angel."

"I know you think I'm a lunatic, Mr. Kincaid, but Nelson is very real! And very soon now you are going to look over your shoulder and find me gone!"

He dropped the firewood in the small area between their two bedrolls. "Try escaping, Miss Diamond, and you'll not only spend the night tied up, you'll ride into Sacramento that way."

"And I don't doubt for one moment that you're capable of just that!"

"Good. I'm glad we understand each other." He crouched down by the pile of wood and began laying out a campfire.

"But that's where you're wrong!" she shouted. "I don't understand you—not at all! I don't understand anybody who would rather think the worst about someone instead of giving them the benefit of the doubt. Is a bounty *that* important to you? Is it worth mistreating an innocent woman?"

He gave her a considering look. "No. But then you're about as innocent as a wolf in a cattle stampede." He struck a match and touched it to the tinder. The wood ignited, and soon the dark clearing was lit up with the orange and red flames of a campfire. "Supper'll be ready in a few minutes."

"And how am I supposed to eat?" Jane demanded.

"I'll free your hands."

"How very generous of you," she retorted. "You must be very frightened of me, a woman half your size."

He gave her a hard glare, telling her she was beginning to get on his nerves, but Jane didn't care—she was fresh *out* of nerves where he and this whole situation were concerned! She glared after him as he went to rummage through his saddlebags. Then he turned back to the fire and crouched by the flames with a can of food and a metal opener in his hand. The opener took the entire top off the can. He poured the contents into a small tin pan, and set the pan on a flat piece of wood in the fire to heat.

A sweet aroma began to fill the air, and Jane's mouth began to water. Her empty stomach became painful again, and it galled her that she was reliant upon Dolan Kincaid for her dinner. If he chose not to feed her, she wouldn't be eating—it was that simple.

Damn that Nelson, anyway. Where was he? She wondered if it was possible for him to untie her while Dolan Kincaid slept. Maybe if the stubborn man woke and found her untied but still there, he'd begin to trust her a little more.

"What are you plotting in that head of yours?" Dolan Kincaid asked from across the fire.

Jane immediately hooded her eyes. "Nothing."

"Uh huh," he said skeptically. "Probably trying to figure out how to get hold of my gun so you can shoot me in the back."

"I hate guns."

"That would explain why you're reputed to be a crack shot."

"I have never fired a gun in my life."

"Good Christ, lady," he said, laughing cynically. "You lie smoother than a snake slithering through water."

"I do not lie!" Jane snapped. "I do not steal, I do not cheat, and I do not *lie!*"

She flinched as he suddenly lurched to his feet and stared up at the night sky. Then he produced a small knife from the back pocket of his jeans, and started toward her.

Jane's eyes rounded. Her time had finally come. He'd finally had enough of her. She pushed back against the tree behind her, her eyes fixed on the tip of the sharp blade shimmering in the firelight. There was a darkness in Dolan Kincaid's blue eyes, an intensity that made her swallow hard as he crouched down beside her.

"Here's the way it's gonna be," he said softly. "I'm going to free your hands. You're going to eat. You move, shuffle, creep, slide, or otherwise budge . . . and I'm going to take your food and replace it with a gag. Do we understand each other?"

Her eyes still on the sharp blade in his hand, Jane nodded slowly.

"And whether or not you lie," he said, leaning so close that his warm breath feathered across her face, "doesn't make a bit of difference. Because I wouldn't believe you one way or the other."

Jane stared into his eyes and then was surprised when his attention slipped down her face to linger on her lips. "It's such a shame," he said softly. "Such a cryin' shame."

While Jane tried to decipher that statement, he slipped his knife between her wrists and cut the knot holding them together. The rope fell away from her hands, and she began rubbing her sore wrists and moving her fingers to work the blood back into them.

And then he did a startling thing: He tucked away his knife, took both of her hands in his, and began rubbing them himself. "I'm sorry it had to be so tight."

"That's . . . that's okay," she replied, staring at his bent head.

His ministrations slowed, and his thumbs began making small, delicate circles on the backs of her hands. And then his eyes lifted to meet hers. Jane felt his gaze like a cyclone in her stomach. "Better?" he asked softly.

She nodded mutely, because she couldn't seem to find her voice.

He nodded back, and then went to the fire to stir their dinner. Jane watched him from the shadows, his tall, muscular body poised in the firelight, his long, dark hair curling down around his neck. He was a handsome man. A handsome, unpredictable, and completely unreasonable man—and any attraction to him on her part would be totally irrational. But here she sat, bound to a tree, waiting for him to feed her, and fascinated by his every move.

"Nelson?" she whispered fiercely. "Where the devil are you?"

She clamped her lips shut and smiled weakly as her virile captor brought her a tin plate filled with baked beans in a thick, rich sauce. The sweet aroma filled Jane's nose, and made her mouth water. She eagerly accepted the metal spoon he offered and shoveled a large bite of beans into her mouth. "You know," she said around a mouthful of food, "if you simply open your mind a little, just long enough to consider what I'm saying—"

"I've always felt it's good to keep an open mind," he interrupted while eating his own dinner, "as long as it's not so open that your brain falls right outta your head."

Jane pursed her lips in frustration, and then turned all her attention on appeasing her hunger. She finished her dinner as Dolan Kincaid was finishing his, and handed him her plate. "It was very good. Thank you."

He arched a dark brow at her. "Well, I'll bet that hurt."

"What's that?"

"That thank-you."

"I'm not an ungrateful person, Mr. Kincaid, when I have things to be grateful *for*. You've kept me safe during our trek through the wilderness, and I do appreciate that. But the fact remains that I wouldn't have needed your efforts at all if you'd come to your senses in the first place and set me free in Pine Oaks."

He smiled at her, bold and bright, and Jane felt a very disconcerting pounding of her heart. "I must be tired," he said, chuckling. "I'm actually beginning to find your attempts to manipulate me entertaining."

He picked up the rope he'd cut from her wrists and held out his hand for hers. Jane stared at his long, tapered fingers, his broad, flat palm, and knew that she had no choice.

She closed her eyes and held out her right hand. This time she was startled at the contact of his fingers: They were warm, gentle with her as he began tying her wrists together again. She kept her eyes closed as he worked, this time refusing to look at the attractive face lingering so close to hers.

For thirty years she'd managed to keep from indulging herself in childish infatuations, knowing they would only bring her heartache in the end. And now here she was, fighting an attraction to a nineteenth-century bounty hunter who was determined to see her hang.

Dolan gave his prisoner a subtle glance from across the campfire. It was late, but she still wasn't asleep. He doubted he'd have been able to fall asleep if he'd been tied like a pagan sacrifice to a pine tree. Still, he refused to feel guilty about tying her up. Making her feel helpless in his hands was a vital part of his plan. He just kept telling himself that she'd be doing herself a favor by helping him—but every time he looked at her against that tree, tired, weak, helpless, his conscience gnawed at him just a bit more. It was time to end this battle and play his trump card.

"Do you intend to sleep tonight?" he asked quietly as he poked at the dwindling fire with a long stick.

"You must be joking," she replied, her voice hoarse with fatigue.

"I suppose the idea of hanging by the neck until dead would keep me awake nights too."

"I won't hang," she stated defensively.

He let out a sardonic laugh. "Don't delude yourself, sweetheart. Hang is what you most certainly will do."

"I'll be rescued by then—"

"By who? Barney and Cleavus?" He grunted. "I wouldn't count on that."

"By Nelson," she retorted.

Christ. Not the angel again. He gave her a direct look. "The only thing that stands a snowball's chance in hell of saving you, lady, is me."

Thankfully that remark caught her attention in just the way he'd hoped. Her head came up and she peered at him intently. "What does that mean?" she asked.

He shrugged and poked at the red-hot embers some more. "It only stands to reason, since I'm the one determined to take you in. Whether you like it or not, I'm the only thing standing between you and a noose."

"Well, that certainly raises my hopes," she remarked.

"You know, if you're lucky, when they pull the lever you'll fall hard enough to snap your neck. Otherwise . . ." He gave a dramatic shudder.

Her eyes rounded in the firelight.

"But I've been thinking, maybe you and I can come to some sort of understanding."

She was quiet for a moment, then asked, "Are you saying you might be willing to let me go?"

Dolan wasn't sure where her acting ended and her true feelings began, but he hoped to high heaven that she was as intrigued by the idea as she seemed.

"No," he replied succinctly.

Her hopeful expression fell.

"But I might be willing to make some sort of deal."

"Deal?" she replied irritably. Her patience with him was obviously wearing as thin as his patience with her.

"I could back you in the tournament."

She squinted at him. "Tournament? What tournament?"

There was no way in hell that she hadn't heard of it— every gambler in the state and beyond worked to earn enough money to enter it each year.

"The Sacramento poker tournament?" he replied indulgently.

"Oh."

"Ever considered entering?"

She gave him a blank look. "No."

Now that surprised him. From all he'd heard about Rose Diamond, she was quite the schemer—always on the lookout for easy money. "I'll take that to mean you've never had the two thousand needed to enter."

"Mr. Kincaid, you can take that any way you like."

Dolan frowned. She wasn't going after the bait the way he'd hoped she would. He supposed he was just going to have to press a little harder.

"I happen to have a little spare cash lying around. I could green stake you. If you win the pot we could split it, sixty-forty."

"The pot?"

"It's expected to be over thirty thousand this year."

Instead of lighting up at the prospect of winning such a large sum of money, she remained unenthused. "Why don't you just play on your own and keep all the money for yourself?"

"Because this tourney attracts some of the best card-players in the country, Miss Diamond. Although I've played my share of cards, I'm not exactly tournament material."

"Oh." She looked down at the ground, seeming to care very little about what he was saying. *How can the woman not jump at this offer?* Dolan thought incredulously. He was giving her a chance to save her foolish neck, and all she had to do was play a few rounds of poker—something she did practically every day of her life!

And then the answer came to him: She wanted more of the winnings. "Look, if I'm going to risk two thousand of my hard-earned dollars to back you in this tourney, then we'll damn well split the pot sixty-forty."

Her answer was a lingering stare in a heavy moment of silence.

"Well?" he finally demanded impatiently.

"So let me get this straight. You're saying that if I play in this tournament, if I play poker . . . then you won't turn me in to the authorities in Sacramento?"

"Lady, I'll set you free and bid you a fond farewell." Thank God she was finally understanding.

"Well." She gave him a tight smile. "That certainly sounds like a fair deal. However we have one small problem."

He frowned. "And what's that?"

"I don't know how to play poker."

A hot burst of anger and frustration shot through Dolan and drove him to his feet. He should have known she wouldn't be so easily manipulated. "Then you've made your choice," he said bitterly. "You'd rather hang."

"Of course not!" she retorted. "There must be something else I can do for you."

Something else? Anger made him circle the fire toward her. Her eyes grew round and large in the dancing firelight as he crouched down beside her. "What else have you got to offer?" he said intently into her face.

Her gaze widened into his. "W-well . . ."

"Maybe a kiss or two?" He sent a scorching glance down to her full breasts beneath the pin-striped cotton of her shirt. "That would do for a start."

She let out a shocked gasp that parted her lush lips. "I . . . Mr. Kincaid, I—"

Driven by both desire and anger, Dolan leaned in and sampled the texture of her full, damp mouth. Her lips parted, tender and soft beneath his, and, although the action was intended to be vengeful, he found that kissing Miss Rose Diamond demanded much more from him than he'd bargained for. His muscles tensed, his heart pounded, his mind raced, and his whole body broke out in a sweat. It was like getting struck in the chest by a thunderbolt, and he pulled back in astonishment. Her eyes were still open, staring into his. She was breathing hard, a pace to match his own, and he quickly tried to remind himself that he was playing a game here, that he was merely trying to manipulate her into doing things his way. But that fact was lost in his aching desire to kiss her one more time.

He took her by the shoulders and leaned toward her once again. Her mouth was warm and soft, yielding beneath his. The kiss was deep, and wet, and lasted half a minute this time before he finally pulled back. He blinked into her startled green eyes, and had a sense that she'd felt the same astonishing sensations he had.

This was the last damn thing he needed. He couldn't afford to let her turn the tables on him like this.

He smiled, ruefully, and shook his head. "Nope. That's not gonna do it. I guess it's the tournament or nothing."

Her expression quickly changed from overwhelmed to indignant. "You— You— How *dare* you take advantage of me when I'm tied helpless to a tree!"

"Lady, that kiss was mutual, and you damn well know it. Now what's it gonna be? A friendly game of cards? Or a deadly game of hangman?"

"Mr. Kincaid, I do not know how to play poker!" she screeched. "I know you don't believe half the things I say, but you're just going to have to take my word on that!"

Dolan gave her a steady glare. This was, apparently, going to be more difficult than he'd expected. "The choice is yours, Miss Diamond," he stated. "I'll expect your answer first thing in the morning."

He ignored her frustrated groan and turned for his bedroll, where he lay down and stretched out for the long night ahead of him. The stars were a blanket of twinkling lights above him as he tried to relax and give the outward appearance that leaving her tied to that tree all night long did nothing to his conscience.

But on the inside he was a mass of churning emotions: frustration, impatience, anger . . . and desire. That kiss had fanned a flame inside of him that he was finding harder and harder to ignore.

She'd agree to the tournament. She had to.

Because if she didn't, he was determined that he would turn her in in Sacramento . . . and let the chips fall where they may.

**9**

*Jane opened her eyes* early the next morning and let out a groan of pain. Her legs were numb, her arms were numb, and her back felt like a hot spike had been driven through it. Despite his irascible nature, she couldn't believe that Dolan Kincaid had left her tied to a tree all night long.

Birds were singing merrily in the trees above as she rotated her head and worked a nasty kink out of her neck. That was when she spotted her captor packing up their horses for another long day in the saddle.

Jane closed her eyes and prayed for a miracle—an earthquake, a flood, pestilence—anything that would prevent her from having to get back up on that horse.

"Good morning," he said darkly, his tone implying something else entirely. There were dark circles beneath his steel-blue eyes, giving Jane the impression that he hadn't slept any better than she had the night before.

*Wonderful,* she thought to herself. Now not only would he be difficult to deal with, he'd be grumpy.

"I don't suppose you could untie me so I can wash up

in the creek." Her voice sounded as tired as her body felt.

He finished with her horse's saddle and strode toward her with his small knife in his hand. The sun through the trees caught on his face as he crouched down to cut her free. He did look tired. But there was something else in his expression as well.

"You've got five minutes," he told her, sawing at the rope.

"Gee, thanks," she grumbled.

The rope fell away and she rubbed the faint marks it had made on her wrists. He leaned closer and began cutting away the rope binding her to the tree.

Jane tried to focus on the shimmer of sun reflecting on the water a few yards away, but the feel of his warm breath on her neck, the powerful magnetism of his simple nearness, was extremely distracting.

Finally, the last rope fell away. Jane leaned gingerly forward, and let out another faint groan as she flexed her stiff back. All of her limbs were tingling and sluggish, and she was only getting five minutes to wash up? It was going to take her at least that long to stand.

She struggled to her knees. And then Dolan held out his hand. "Let me help you."

Jane stared at his gesture. Her gaze shifted to his face. Did she miss her guess, or was that guilt she saw mirrored in his slightly hooded eyes?

She accepted his hand, and found that she wasn't any more immune to the warmth of his touch than she was to his simple nearness. She allowed Dolan to slowly pull her to her feet, and rose up in front of him, their bodies mere inches apart. He stared down into her face. She looked up into his. And in that moment Jane actually found herself longing for him to kiss her again. In her life, she'd never experienced anything quite so exciting, quite so titillating as the kiss they'd shared the night before.

He moved closer. Her heart nearly stopped as his lips came within a breath of hers. "Five minutes, Miss Diamond," he reiterated. "Not a second more."

Jane jerked back from him, feeling foolish and hurt. "I heard you the first time, Mr. Kincaid. It's my abused body that needs medical attention, not my ears."

She attempted to brush past him but he caught her by the arm. "You be sure to let me know when you've made up your mind."

She yanked free from his grasp. "Made up my mind about what?"

"About saving your own foolish neck."

The tournament again. "I gave you my answer last night, Mr. Kincaid. I haven't the slightest idea how to play poker."

"You're being very foolish, Miss Diamond."

"You're being very pigheaded, Mr. Kincaid."

He narrowed his eyes. "Well, well. It seems you've got a temper in there after all."

"Everyone has their limits."

"I agree."

She grunted. "Well, I won't get too used to *that* happening."

"You've just wasted two of your minutes, Miss Diamond."

Jane stared hard at him. "More like two days," she shot back.

"It hasn't been any picnic for me either, lady," he retorted, heading back to the horses.

"At least you're here by choice, Mr. Kincaid. Try being abandoned by an angel and then kidnapped by a lunatic!"

"Christ," he muttered. "Get yourself moving. Your trial awaits," he added with a vindictive sneer.

Every muscle in Jane's body suddenly went tense, and she found she couldn't move. Anger, white and hot, was building inside her—taking her over like an alien being.

She had been dragged through the wilderness, yelled at, shot at, jailed, shot at *some more*, and then tied to a tree for one solid, harrowing night. She'd turned the other cheek so many times in the past two days that she was practically spinning in a tight circle. Jane Baker had had enough! She threw back her shoulders, stuck out her chin, and strode toward the man who was, in her opinion, responsible for every moment of misfortune she'd experienced since arriving in the nineteenth century. She glared up into his eyes.

"My name," she began tightly, "is Jane Baker. Then she leaned closer and shouted into his face, *"Did you get that, Dolan Kincaid! My name is Jane Baker!* And if you," she added, jabbing him hard in the chest, "don't stop calling me Miss Diamond . . . I am going to shove a pine tree so far up your backside you'll be able to pick your teeth with it!"

He studied her quietly for a moment, while Jane huffed and puffed and tried to catch her breath: This confrontation stuff was exhausting! "Now you've wasted three minutes," he finally said.

She tensed her hands into fists—to keep from going for his throat. *"Ahhhhh!!"* she screamed. "I have *had* it with your bossiness! And I am sick to *death* of dealing with your lack of faith! You've got a definite personality problem, mister—"

"At least I've *got* a personality! I don't have to resort to pretending to be somebody else to get what I want!"

"I am *not* pretending!"

"Oh, save it for the judge. You'll be meeting him in about eight hours."

Jane gritted her teeth. "If you think I'm getting back up on that horse, you are sadly mistaken, Mr. Kincaid. I'd rather *walk* to Sacramento."

"You'll either sit in that saddle, or be slung over it, face first."

"*That* would probably be more comfortable!"

"Well, it can be arranged!"

"I only wonder what's stopped you from doing that before! Not a conscience—we both know you don't have one of those!"

The muscles in his jaw tensed. "You've just bitched your way down to one minute."

"Which is about how long it would take for you to recite your morals, Mr. Kincaid. With time to spare, I'm sure." She squared her shoulders again. "Now. I intend to take as long as necessary at the creek. It will be up to you to *drag* me away when you feel my allotted time is up. Frankly," she added as she turned away from him, "I wouldn't expect anything less from a man like you."

With that, she marched off toward the water. She'd never met a more irritating human being in all of her life—and where in God's name was that damn angel?!

"Nelson," she hissed, picking her way over the rocky beach. "Strap on your dented halo and get yourself front and center!"

But the angel didn't appear. Considering her luck lately, Jane hadn't really expected that he'd come winging her way simply because she called him.

Careful of her sore legs, she knelt by the water's edge and rinsed out her mouth. She splashed cold water over her face, washing away the dirt and grime of two long days in the saddle.

She caught her reflection in the clear water, and it told a very sad story. Her face was sunburned, and her hair was a mess of tangles: half of it hanging limply in her face; the other half struggling valiantly to stay in a ponytail. She tugged out the elastic band and pushed her fingers through her hair, giving it a good shake, and sending it in a cascade down her back and over her shoulders.

She dunked her head beneath the surface of the cold water and gave her scalp a good, invigorating scrub with her fingernails. Then she sat back on her heels and pushed her fingers through her wet, dripping tresses.

"Let's go," Dolan Kincaid commanded from the campsite. Jane calmly looked up at the clear blue sky and enjoyed the sound of the breeze blowing through the leafy trees. She refused to jump just because Dolan Kincaid said so. "I don't suppose you made any coffee?" she called.

"No time for breakfast. Not if we wanna reach Sacramento by nightfall. We'll eat hardtack on the trail."

She cast him a baleful glance over her shoulder. "Yet another great reason for me to smile this morning."

"Miss Baker. Don't we look all refreshed."

Jane turned back toward the creek and found Nelson standing before her, his Italian leather loafers poised, miraculously, above the gently flowing water of the creek.

"Well, it's about time," she snapped. "Can I assume,

from that absurd smile of yours, that you have finally figured this mess out?"

The angel gave her an up-down glance and brushed a piece of imaginary lint off the double-breasted jacket of his immaculate white suit. "We've apparently gotten up on the wrong side of the bed this morning."

"Bed?" Jane retorted. "What bed? *I* spent the night tied to a damn tree! Where the hell have you been?"

"I have been researching, nonstop, trying to come up with a solution to our little dilemma. How are you holding up?"

"*Not at all*," Jane replied tightly. "This entire situation is . . . is *completely*—"

She suddenly found herself grabbed from behind and yanked to her feet. "Who the hell are you talking to?" Dolan Kincaid demanded as he spun her around, wrapped his strong arm around her waist, and hauled her up tightly against his chest. He had his gun held at the ready while he stared into the thick underbrush on the other side of the creek.

"Good heavens," Nelson exclaimed, his tiny blue eyes as round as walnuts. "Don't the men in this day and age *bathe?* Unhand her, you stubble-faced brute, before I'm forced to take a bar of soap to you!"

Jane supposed she would have appreciated Nelson's gallant threat a bit more if Mr. Kincaid were capable of hearing it. As it was, it was up to her to calm the suspicious bounty hunter down. But first she had to battle her own reaction to his nearness, which was substantial, to say the very least; his odd effect on her seemed to be growing stronger by the minute. She took a deep breath to calm her racing heart, and braced her hands against his rock-hard chest. "Mr. Kincaid, it's not—"

"Barney!" he bellowed over her head. "Cleavus! You two fellas still interested in meeting the mean end of my gun?"

Nelson, standing not two feet in front of Dolan, blinked and leaned to one side. "Why is this man yelling at me?"

"He isn't yelling *at* you, he's yelling *through* you. He thinks there are two men across the creek attempting to rescue me. Mr. Kincaid, I am not talking to Barney and Cleavus. I'm talking to Nelson. He has finally returned—with good news, I hope," she added, giving the angel a pointed glare.

"This man *knows* about me?" Nelson replied, flabbergasted.

"I told him about you yesterday."

"Great," Dolan muttered. He released her and reholstered his gun. "The angel again. You're just hell-bent on driving me nuts, aren't you?"

Nelson arched a pale brow. "And what, exactly, is that supposed to mean?"

"I said I told him about you, Nelson. I didn't say he believed me."

Dolan snorted. "I believe in a lot of things, sweetheart, but fairies aren't one of 'em."

Nelson's pale face turned red. "I *beg* your pardon, sir, but I am no *fairy*. I am a bona fide, certified, double-documented angel. Not that there's anything *wrong* with fairies," he added magnanimously.

"He's an angel, Mr. Kincaid," Jane explained flippantly. "*Not* a fairy."

"Angels. Fairies. Hell, it's too early in the morning for this shit."

Nelson gasped at the expletive. "Good lord, what a

cad! Miss Baker, it *completely* escapes me why you would wish to remain in this man's company."

Now it was Jane's turn to be affronted, and she turned away from her virile captor to plant a drilling glare on Nelson. "I do *not* wish to remain in Mr. Kincaid's company. I *wish* to return home."

"All right, enough already," Dolan Kincaid said. He took her by the arm and began leading her back to the horses.

Jane dragged her feet. "My backside won't take another day in a saddle, Nelson!" she called. "Now I'm done with this waiting game! I want out of here—I want out of here *right now*!"

"Wonderful," Nelson replied, clapping his hands. He glanced around the creek. "Now all we need is a nice tall cliff. . . ."

"No! No cliffs! No racing wagons, no speeding bullets, no raging rivers! I absolutely, indisputably refuse to *die* again!"

In that instant something went whizzing past Jane's head and she let out a startled cry. Dolan Kincaid let out a colorful curse—which pulled yet another affronted gasp out of Nelson—and Jane found herself shoved behind the bounty hunter's broad back.

"Good heavens!" Nelson exclaimed. "*Who,* pray tell, are *they*?"

Jane peeked around Dolan Kincaid's broad shoulders, expecting to see Barney and Cleavus standing there in the glare of the sunlight, but her eyes widened on two buckskin-clad Indians standing across the creek. Their bows were pulled taut, ready to let more deadly arrows fly. And they were aiming directly at her and Dolan.

"Nelson?" she squeaked, casting a panicked glance at the angel.

Nelson broke into a mischievous smile. "Well, well, Miss Baker," he said, rocking back on his heels. "How, may I ask, do you feel about piercing arrows?"

Dolan couldn't believe his luck.

After planning for months to win that poker tourney, he was being thwarted by a woman who refused to admit who she really was, a pair of bungling outlaws who didn't know when to give up, an imaginary angel who insisted he wasn't a fairy, and now he had renegade Indians staring him in the face.

"That's not funny, Nelson!" Rose Diamond shouted.

She was standing behind him, her small hands clutching at the back of his shirt. For someone so unwilling to die, she sure the hell was pushing her luck.

"For God's sake, Miss Diamond"—Dolan gritted his teeth—"shut the hell up." She was going to end up getting them *both* killed. He kept his eyes on the bows and arrows being directed at them from across the creek, and considered his options. These were renegades, Paiute if he didn't miss his guess, and renegades had one goal in life: rape, pillage—destroy—the whites. He could always draw his gun, take his chances that he could kill them both before either got off an arrow. Aw hell, he was fast, but he wasn't *that* fast. The one left standing would kill him—and he didn't even want to think about what would then happen to the woman standing behind him.

"I won't do it!" Rose Diamond cried. "A *bullet* would be better than this!"

If she didn't keep her mouth closed, Dolan was going to gladly accommodate her. Taking a bullet would be a far better death than what these two had in store for them anyway.

The renegades' obsidian black eyes were fixed and intent, like two wild animals sizing up their prey. Dolan realized that he had no choice but to submit—for the moment—and he slowly raised his hands away from his gun.

"Just stay very still," he advised the woman behind him.

"Would you stop babbling at me!" she blurted.

"I am just trying to keep us both from being slaughtered," Dolan retorted.

"I am *not* talking to you, Mr. Kincaid!"

The two renegades narrowed their eyes and fingered their bowstrings. A warm breeze sifted through the surrounding trees and flapped at their buckskin breeches, and Dolan figured that was probably the last breath of wind he'd ever feel on his face.

"Damn it, Nelson!" Rose Diamond shouted. "There has to be another way!"

Dolan, keeping his hands benignly in the air, gave the renegades a hesitant smile. "Miss Diiiamond," he sang through his teeth. "Now is not the tiiime."

"Furthermore, I do *not* appreciate your tone! While you've been sitting up in heaven, twiddling your thumbs, I have been tied up, locked up, knocked down, shot at, sunburned, half-starved, and now"—she gestured past Dolan at the renegades—"now, I've got Indians flinging arrows at me!"

"Easy, fellas," Dolan soothed. "The heat's just gettin' to the lady a bit."

"Yes, Nelson, they probably are going to kill me. And then won't *you* be pleased?"

"Miss Diamond, for a person so set against dying," Dolan growled, "you sure are running fast toward—"

"Well, that's not much of a choice!" she snapped. "What kind of angel are you?! Oh, just go away, Nelson! GO AWAY!"

Dolan gave a quick, sharp glance over his shoulder. "Lady, there are two Indians standing not twenty feet away with the firm intention of killing us both. I suggest you knock this shit off and shut the hell up!"

*"Enough already!"* she cried. And then, amazingly enough, she stepped out from behind his back and faced the Indians head-on. "I just can't *take* this any longer!"

Dolan tried to step back in front of her, to block her with his body, but the damn fool woman kept dancing around him like a goddamn ballerina.

The renegades, meanwhile, were beginning to look a bit nervous.

Rose Diamond was apparently determined to die. She threw back her head and held her arms akimbo. "Hurry up before I lose my nerve!" she shouted.

"Christ!" Dolan took her by the waist and spun her around, trying to make her less of a target. "What the hell are you doing?!"

He looked hesitantly back at the renegades, and paused at what he saw: The Indians were backing away, slowly. And then they spun around and ran into the woods as if the devil himself were at their heels.

Rose Diamond twisted from Dolan's grasp as he stood there staring in disbelief. The woman had just scared two bloodthirsty Indians half to death.

"What just happened here?" she demanded. "Where are they going?"

Dolan crossed his arms over his chest and smiled broadly. "It seems your acting finally came in handy, Miss Diamond. They thought you were crazy."

"*Crazy?*" she repeated, staring in the direction the Indians had run.

"It's very bad medicine to kill a crazy person."

"But I'm *not* crazy," she retorted.

"That's debatable." He gave her a sidelong glance, and found her expression so absolutely dumbfounded that it was comical. And he started to laugh.

She gave him a dark look, which only made him laugh harder. "I don't see what's so funny," she remarked.

"I kept trying to . . . to protect you!" Dolan stammered in between breaths. "But . . . but you kept . . . kept . . . "

She was staring at him as if *he* were the lunatic. "I was trying to get killed, Mr. Kincaid. I didn't *want* you to protect me—what is so blasted funny?!"

"You!" he burst out. He imitated her martyr stance with her head thrown back and her arms outstretched. "Hell, I woulda . . . woulda run from ya too!"

A smile twitched on her lips. "I suppose I did look a little strange standing there begging to be shot."

He nodded. He was now laughing so hard his eyes were watering.

And then Rose started to laugh. The sound started out soft and melodic, and then grew into gut-wrenching peals until the entire clearing was echoing with the sound of their combined laughter.

A few minutes later Dolan managed to regain his composure. "Come on," he said. "Let's get outta here before they rethink their retreat and come back."

Though she was still giggling, Rose's eyes rounded. "They'd do that?"

He chuckled. "Stranger things have sure the hell happened."

She nodded and moved toward her horse. "Thank you for saddling him up for me."

He gave her a surprised glance. "You're welcome."

She smiled at him, and his chest tightened. He couldn't seem to take his eyes off her as she shook out her wet hair and prepared to mount up.

He could see one of the reasons the woman was such a talented poker player; she could be quite a distraction and would likely make any man playing opposite her lose complete track of the game.

But Dolan couldn't afford to experience the same sort of distraction. If he intended to coerce her into that poker game by the end of the day, then he'd need to keep thinking clearly where she was concerned.

He turned toward his horse. And in that moment something cracked him painfully on the back of the head and sent him spiraling into unconsciousness.

# 10

 

 

*Jane stared at her large brown horse,* and wavered at the daunting task of mounting it on her own. "Mr. Kincaid," she called, "could you possibly help me—" She turned to find Barney Rollins and Cleavus Coltrain standing by Dolan's horse, grinning like fools. Dolan Kincaid was lying in a heap at their feet.

Jane let out a sharp cry and rushed toward him.

"We got him, Miss Rose!" Cleavus stated proudly. "We finally got him!"

"What did you do?" she demanded, dropping to her knees beside Dolan. There didn't seem to be any blood, but the man was out colder than a drunk at dawn.

"We gave him a good whack on the head," Barney replied, gesturing with his gun. He sniffed confidently. "You want I should finish him off for ya?"

Jane glared up at the two men. "I thought I'd seen the last of you two in the meadow."

"Well, now, w-we can explain that, Miss Rose," Barney stammered. "Ya . . . ya see, we w-was going for reinforcements."

"Yeah, yeah," Cleavus nodded eagerly. "Reinforcements."

"Oh please," Jane retorted. It was obvious that these two were cowards, from their dusty hats, right down to the tips of their muddy boots. "You two ran off to save your own necks and left me there to fend for myself. No wonder Rose Diamond treats you so shabbily—you don't deserve any better!"

Cleavus broke into a grin. "Hey, she's yellin' at us, Barn. She must be feelin' better."

"I bet you two stood back there in those woods just now and watched those Indians almost *kill* me and Mr. Kincaid."

"Now that's not fair at all," Barney defended. "We . . . we didn't wanna come chargin' out and spook 'em more than they already were."

"'Sides," Cleavus added, breaking into another grin, "we knew you'd take care a things just fine, Miss Rose."

Barney snickered. "You shore did show them Injuns what for."

"Yeah." Cleavus snorted. "They hightailed it outta here like a couple a women."

Dolan Kincaid's hand twitched, and the two men jumped about ten feet into the air. "Whoa!" Barney exclaimed. "We best get on outta here while the gettin's good."

Jane rose to her feet. "I agree." She gave them a clipped wave. "Good-bye."

Cleavus gaped at her. "But . . . but, Miss Rose. Ain't you comin' with us?"

"No—and don't even *think* about tying me up in that saddle again. I am staying *right* where I am, and I want you two to stop these ridiculous attempts to rescue me.

Now, turn around. Get on your horses. *And go the hell away!"*

"B-but—" Barney began.

Jane pointed at their horses, which were wading through the cool creek a few yards away. "Go!" she commanded. Both men stumbled backward, and then hurried to their horses. They struggled into their saddles, gave Jane one last baffled look, and then raced off into the woods.

Jane didn't think she'd ever shouted so much in her life as she had that morning. Her throat was sore and her nerves were raw as she sank down once again beside where Dolan Kincaid lay sprawled on the ground.

"Miss Baker . . . may I make a suggestion?"

Jane glanced up to find Nelson standing directly in front of her. She hadn't forgotten the way he'd nagged at her while a pair of murderous Indians were stalking her; the angel would be lucky if she ever spoke to him again.

"Run," he said simply.

She gave him a hard stare. "What?"

"Run far, run fast. Ride the blasted horse if you have to, just get out of here before that man regains consciousness."

Jane looked down into Dolan's face. He looked so peaceful lying there in the sunlight. "I am not going to leave this man battered and broken in the middle of the wilderness. He could need medical attention."

"Miss Baker," Nelson began impatiently. "As I told you earlier, I have been busy researching our little problem. While I haven't come up with any feasible answers—other than the one I've already told you about—which, again, I must say is extremely reasonable considering the circumstances—"

"Nelson, I seriously doubt you'd think dying was all

that reasonable if it were you being goaded to jump off the nearest cliff."

He pursed his lips. "Be that as it may, Miss Baker, I have come to the conclusion that it could take me at least another two days to come up with any concrete solutions in this matter—"

"Two days!" Jane exclaimed, leaping to her feet. "We'll reach Sacramento by nightfall! He's going to have me locked up! I'm . . . I'm going to have to stand trial before Hanging Judge Colfax—"

"All the more reason to *run*, Miss Baker," he urged. "You have no other recourse at this point."

Jane looked down at Dolan once again. The idea of leaving him there, hurt and unconscious, left a pit the size of Texas in her stomach. And an action like that would only solidify the suspicions he'd had about her all along, that she was heartless and completely untrustworthy.

And how great were her chances of surviving an escape attempt? Unlike Dolan, she had no idea how to make her way through this dense wilderness. She doubted she'd survive one night alone.

However she couldn't overlook the fact that by the end of the day he intended to turn her in to the authorities, where she'd be locked up in jail to stand trial in the morning. She supposed she had a choice to make, between the lesser of two evils.

Unless . . .

"I'm not running away, Nelson."

"Miss Baker, for God's sake, listen to reason! As much as I hope for your physical demise at this point, I'd rather it not be in front of a bloodthirsty, beer-swilling crowd with a rope around your neck!"

"I have another idea."

"What, pray tell, could you have possibly come up—"

She smiled at him. "You're just going to have to trust me, Nelson."

The angel rolled his eyes. "Goody."

Dolan Kincaid groaned and finally opened his eyes. He squinted up at her through the glaring sunlight. "What the hell happened?" his voice rasped.

"Are you all right, Mr. Kincaid?"

He blinked, and refocused on her face. "Did you . . . did you *hit* me?"

"It wasn't me," she said, bending to help him to his feet. "It was Barney and Cleavus."

Dolan spun around quickly, as if preparing for a fight, and wavered slightly on his feet. "Ah," he moaned, pressing his hand to the back of his head. "Where are the sons a bitches?"

"They're gone. And I told them not to come back."

He gave her the starkest look of confusion Jane had ever seen. "You what?"

"I'm tired of them popping up and causing problems—"

"How long was I out?"

"About five minutes."

His blue eyes narrowed. "Then why the hell are you still here?"

Astounded, Jane looked at Nelson, who crossed his arms and gave her an I-told-you-so look. "You don't honestly believe I would leave you here, hurt and unconscious?"

"Frankly, lady, I don't know *what* the hell to believe about you anymore."

"Well, believe *this*, Mr. Kincaid, I could have not only

left you here, I could have had those two pea-brains shoot you right there where you lay! But I am *not* the coldhearted criminal you think I am!"

He winced, touching his fingers to the back of his head again. "Could you stop shouting? You're making my head hurt."

"I'm sorry," she offered begrudgingly. "Let me take a look at it."

He bent his head down and she sifted through the back of his thick hair. "You're lucky your head is so hard," she grumbled, to distract herself as she did such an intimate thing. It felt good touching him—too good. "It could have been cracked wide open."

"Hell, it feels like it *was*."

"You've got quite a goose egg back here. The skin's broken a little." She stepped away from him. "But it doesn't look too serious."

He picked up his hat, dusted it off, and pulled it down onto his head. "Still fits," he said with a vague smile.

Jane nodded, still recovering from the tingling sensations caused by simply touching him.

He stared at her for a moment, as if he had something more to say but didn't quite know how to get it out. Finally he hooked his thumbs in his gun belt and stared down at his boots. "Thank you."

Jane couldn't control a smile. "Well, I bet that hurt," she replied, repeating his words to her from the night before.

"I can't help but wonder what you'll expect in return for your *generosity*."

Jane shook her head. It would make things so much easier if the stubborn man would stop thinking the worst of her all the time. "Mr. Kincaid, I've changed my mind."

He gave her a suspicious look. "Changed your mind about what?"

"Your deal."

"Really," he said carefully.

"Really." She stuck out her hand to him. "You've got yourself a poker player."

He stared at her hand for a moment, probably trying to determine whether or not she was being honest with him. Then his gaze rose to meet hers. "Sixty-forty?"

"Sixty-forty."

He nodded once, grasped her small hand in his, and smiled. "Miss Diamond, you've just avoided yourself a hanging and gotten rich in the process."

Jane smiled back hesitantly. She'd bought herself some time, but she sincerely hoped that Nelson had her home before the poker tournament started. Otherwise Mr. Dolan Kincaid was likely to hang her himself.

Poker. The woman was going to play poker?

Nelson leaned back in his leather office chair and sighed heavily. To the best of his knowledge Miss Jane Baker had never even *held* a deck of cards, let alone played in any tournaments.

Why hadn't she just run off when he'd urged her to? The way she'd looked at the unconscious Mr. Kincaid, all soft and dewy-eyed, almost made him believe that she was nursing feelings for the ruffian.

Nelson suddenly lunged forward in his chair. "Good heavens," he rasped. "She wouldn't—she *couldn't*!"

But women falling in love with their captors was a very common phenomenon. And Miss Jane Baker was a very naive, very susceptible young woman. Why, if she fancied herself in love with this Kincaid character, she might not *ever* want to return home. How in God's name would he explain *that* to Stella?

Nelson lifted his chin determinedly. For his own sake as well as his client's, it was time for him to start playing hardball.

Jane glanced up from the narrow, winding trail ahead of her to watch a bald eagle screech across the cornflower blue sky. Considering the way her day had been going, she wouldn't have been the least bit surprised if the giant bird had dived down and lifted her right out of her saddle. She'd had nothing but one calamity after another.

Not one hour into their journey, something had spooked her horse and sent it rearing up on its hind legs. Jane had gone tumbling to the ground, but, luckily, she'd landed in a patch of ferns, which had broken her fall—or she might have broken her neck.

And then, not ten minutes after she'd mounted back up and headed back down the trail behind Mr. Kincaid, a boulder the size of a car had come barreling down a cliffside toward her. If her horse hadn't already been skittish from the earlier scare, it might not have been wary enough to dance out of the way before the boulder steamrolled off the side of the hill.

After that, there had been a thick branch from an overhanging tree that had suddenly come flying at her head. Dolan had shouted just in time to make Jane duck, and the branch had narrowly missed hitting her. Then there was the rattlesnake—her poor horse had been a bundle of nerves by then. Luckily Jane held on tightly that time, and managed to remain in the saddle.

She was wondering what could possibly happen next as she lifted her face into the gentle breeze that was keeping her cool beneath the hot sun. Dolan had been strangely quiet since starting out that morning. Jane would have thought her agreeing to his card game would have at least made him a bit more friendly toward her. But it seemed to have had the exact opposite effect.

Regardless, Jane had been doing her best to draw him into conversation, but he was being very stingy with his company.

"So, how long have you been a bounty hunter?" she called to him, adjusting her position in her saddle. That morning she'd been surprised to discover that she wasn't at all as sore as she'd been the day before; she assumed her nerve endings had given up the fight.

"'Bout ten years," he answered.

"In this day and age it must be very easy for a criminal to evade justice," she replied.

His back stiffened minutely, and she realized she'd just insulted him.

"I mean, with no fingerprinting system, no DNA testing, no identification technique except simple human sight, the criminals must really have it made." She rolled her eyes, knowing she was just making things worse with her rambling.

"Right," he responded.

She had to stop talking as if she were from the future; those kind of comments only irritated Dolan and reminded him of how maniacal he thought she was.

"Well." She let out a faint laugh, and urged her horse up alongside his. She was actually getting the hang of controlling the animal on her own. "I believe *I* can attest to the fact that you do your job very well, Mr. Kincaid."

He gave her a vague smile and their gazes locked. Jane found herself drowning in his eyes in the midst of a heavy silence.

A few moments later they broke their stare simultaneously, cleared their throats in unison, and redirected their attention to the trail ahead.

"How, um, how much longer until we arrive?" Jane asked, pretending that their almost physical connection had never happened.

"'Bout four hours."

Another long, uncomfortable silence followed as their horses lumbered on beneath them.

"Is that where you're from? Sacramento, I mean?"

"Nope. Nebraska."

"Oh. Do you still have family there?"

"I never did."

She smiled. "What do you mean, you never did? Were you hatched from an egg?"

"Both of my parents died before I was six."

"Oh."

Silence again reigned as their horses picked along the trail. "So what about you?"

Jane gave him a startled look. This was the first time he'd initiated a conversation with her all day. "Me?"

"What makes you tick?"

Jane shrugged. "A decided lack of self-confidence, I suppose." He broke into deep laughter. "That wasn't meant to be funny, Mr. Kincaid."

"Lady, the woman I've spent the past three days with is hardly lacking in self-confidence. You've dodged bullets, scared off Indians, even held your own against me—which I'm told is quite a feat in itself."

Jane blinked in surprise. He was right. She had done all those things. Just three days ago she would have buried her head in the sand at the very thought of going through what she'd been forced to endure since arriving in the nineteenth century. But she'd handled each crisis with a relatively cool head, and an unusually competent demeanor. She supposed she was stronger than she'd ever given herself credit for.

"So what's the real story on Rose Diamond?" Dolan pressed.

Jane had no idea what the real story was on Rose Diamond, but she wasn't about to ruin the first real conversation she'd had with Dolan all day by mentioning that point. "I'm an orphan of sorts too. My father died when I was sixteen, and my mother died just last year."

"Where did you grow up?"

"Here, in California. You?"

"An orphanage."

Jane blinked in surprise. He'd spent his childhood in an orphanage? The idea made her very sad, and she found she had to fight a sudden urge to reach out and touch him. She clutched the pommel in front of her instead. "That must have been very lonely for you."

He laughed again, a sound she found she was beginning to enjoy. "I was constantly surrounded by fifty other kids. I swore that when I got out of there I'd find a place where I could be alone."

"Well, you certainly found that out here," she replied, looking off into the dense trees and heavy foliage surrounding them.

"Yeah, but eventually every man needs a place he can call home."

She gave him a surprised glance. "Now that sounds

suspiciously like a man rethinking his job choice."

He shrugged. "Riding the range can get old after a while." He raised his arms above his head and stretched out his strong back. "So can sleeping on the cold, hard ground. But it takes money to start over in this world. After we win this tournament, my bounty huntin' days'll be over. I assume you'll take your forty percent and head for Mexico?"

Jane nodded distractedly. She hadn't really heard anything he'd said after he'd admitted to her his reasons for wanting the tournament money. She was suddenly feeling very guilty. She was risking this man's dreams for her own selfish needs. She had to give reasoning with him one more try. "Mr. Kincaid? There's . . . there's something I really need to tell you."

He turned those deep blue eyes of his on her and Jane almost lost her train of thought. "What is it?" he prompted.

She took a deep breath. "The . . . the truth is that I—"

"Wait. Wait a minute. If you're about to go off on another of your tangents about not being Rose Diamond, about not knowing how to play poker, of being from the future, of talking to angels—or any of those in any particular order, *don't*. Spare us both, Miss Diamond."

"But, Mr. Kincaid—"

"No buts," he said firmly. "Let's just have a nice, quiet ride from here on out."

Jane rolled her eyes and turned her attention to the trail ahead. The man was so pigheaded he was going to bring about his own downfall. She only wished there were some way she really *could* win him that money.

Jane was working on an idea a few minutes later,

when she felt herself slowly beginning to slide to the left. Bewildered, she looked down at the horse beneath her, which was grunting in disapproval.

"What the—"

That was all Dolan Kincaid was able to get out before Jane's saddle went south—with her in it. She let out a cry of surprise, unable to grab hold of anything that would keep her mounted. Luckily she was riding right beside Dolan at the time and he reached out with his strong arms and swept her up onto his lap just as her heavy saddle hit the ground.

She clung to his neck as he held her tightly to his chest. "I checked that cinch myself this morning," he said. Jane took a deep breath, to calm her pounding heart.

"It's not your fault," she said.

"You're shaking. Are you all right?"

"I'm . . . I'm . . ." Jane wanted to answer, but her tongue seemed to get tangled up around her teeth. Her eyes locked with Dolan's and she couldn't seem to break away.

He brushed her hair back from her face. "You've had quite an eventful day," he said softly. "Your sunburn looks a little better though."

"It . . . feels better," she managed to get out.

"Your lips still look a . . . a little red." He tentatively leaned forward, and then kissed her gently, his full lips clinging briefly to hers. "Does that hurt?" he asked.

Her eyes round, Jane jerked her head in the basic motion of "no."

He leaned close again and kissed her once more, and this time Jane felt the warm glide of his tongue over her lips. Her stomach leaped, causing her to gasp, which caused her to open her mouth. And Dolan Kincaid took that as an invitation to deepen their kiss.

Jane didn't know what to do as his tongue swept into her mouth. She'd never been kissed like this before. She clung to his broad shoulders, praying she wouldn't do something ridiculous like fall right off his lap to the ground below.

When he finally released her, she stared, startled, into his warm blue eyes while her heart raced like a freight train in her chest. He'd kissed her like a man who desired her, like a man who was actually enjoying their embrace.

"Why did . . . you do that?" she asked in a faint rasp.

"Because I wanted to."

She gave him a shy smile. "You did?"

He laughed and shook his head. "I swear, sometimes you seem more like a schoolgirl than a first-rate cardsharp."

Jane had no comment to that as he lifted her off his lap and set her on her feet on the ground. Then he dismounted, picked up her fallen saddle, and set it back on her horse's back. He frowned as he checked her cinch buckle.

"Did it break?" she asked.

He shook his head. "Nope. It just worked loose somehow. Damnedest thing I've ever seen." He cinched the saddle back on, making sure it was nice and tight, and then turned toward Jane.

She caught her breath as he took her firmly around the waist and lifted her back into her saddle. "Does it feel snug?" he asked.

She shifted her weight from side to side, and then nodded.

He turned to his horse and swung powerfully up into

his own saddle. Jane's heart was still racing in her chest. In fact, she didn't think it would ever slow down again. Dolan had kissed her because he'd wanted to—not because he'd been trying to intimidate her or prove some kind of point. He'd simply wanted to.

As they headed off down the trail once again, Jane broke into a broad smile. Dolan Kincaid was beginning to like her. And the idea made her feel tingly all over.

**11**

Jane flipped her damp hair over the curved rim of the brass tub, leaned back into the warm water until it lapped against her chin, sighed, and closed her eyes. She'd spent the past thirty minutes ensconced in her stateroom aboard the *Lady Gambler*, scrubbing herself from head to toe with a soft cloth. After three long days in the dust and hot sun, she finally felt clean.

She looked over at the green velvet gown draped across the foot of her bed and smiled—she'd done little else but smile since her and Dolan's kiss earlier that day. She'd found the beautiful gown tucked down in Rose Diamond's saddlebags, along with several other items— including a rose-scented bar of soap. She'd had the dress pressed by a steward, and was now looking forward to dressing for her dinner with Dolan.

"I don't suppose I should ask what you're daydreaming about."

Startled, Jane sloshed water onto the polished wood of the floor as she quickly folded her arms over her bare chest. Though well past eight in the evening, the lavishly furnished stateroom was cast in a golden glow from the light of the two hurricane lanterns placed on either side of the wrought-iron bed. They illuminated Nelson's pale face as he leaned against her closed door.

"Nelson!" she cried.

"You used to be a perfectly sensible woman, before Mr. Dolan Kincaid barged into your life."

"Get out of here!" she demanded, sinking lower into her soapy bathwater.

"And now I doubt God Himself could talk sense into you."

"If you've come to try and talk me into killing myself again, then you're wasting your breath," she stated.

"And you, my dear, are wasting precious time. Rose Diamond is destined to hang any day now—"

"I am *not* Rose Diamond!"

"As far as the people around here are concerned, you most certainly are."

"But Dolan isn't going to turn me in—"

The angel arched a brow. "*Dolan,* is it? You know, Miss Baker, cultivating an attraction for him will only bring you heartache in the end. The man will be dead and moldering before you're even born."

"I am *not* trying to cultivate an attraction for Mr. Kincaid. I am simply trying my best to avoid being *hanged.* I'm certainly not getting a whole lot of help from *you!*"

Nelson pursed his lips. "I have spent the entire *day* trying to help you, Miss Baker. I tried everything short of incineration, and you simply *refuse* to die!"

All of the day's dangerous mishaps came back to Jane and she let out an astounded gasp. "You?! Dear God, my own guardian angel has spent the entire day trying to kill me!"

"I have been trying to *help* you," he retorted.

"Then please, for God's sake, stop!"

"Oh, you people on this earth are so ungrateful for the time and hard work we angels put in on your behalf."

"Stop harping and turn around so I can get out of this tub. I'm already running late for the tournament dinner."

Nelson did as she asked and presented her with his back. "Miss Baker," he said in a more reasonable tone. "There must be something I can say to convince you to give up on this ridiculous poker tournament."

Jane reached for the towel she'd left lying on the floor and stood from the water. "I don't happen to think it's so ridiculous."

"You seem to be forgetting one small fact."

"Which is?"

"You wouldn't know a poker hand if it crawled up your neck and bit you on the nose!"

"I'm working on that," she said evasively. She finished drying herself and her hair and reached for her dress.

"Really," he mocked. "Well, I hope you're working on your final prayers as well, because Mr. Kincaid is going to shoot you right between the eyes when he finds out you've tricked him."

"I haven't *tricked* him," she replied defensively, buttoning up the side of her gown. "I have every intention of helping him to the best of my ability."

"Which isn't saying much," Nelson grumbled.

"You know, for an angel you're very pessimistic."

"Realistic, Miss Baker. *Realistic.*"

"You can turn around now."

Nelson turned, took one look at her, and his jaw dropped. Jane decided to take that as a compliment.

She stepped in front of the cheval glass and smiled at her reflection. She'd gone through nothing short of an amazing transformation in the past few days. Her face was tanned a soft golden hue, and a faint smattering of freckles was scattered across the bridge of her nose.

She reached up and shook out her hair, which was drying fast in the warmth of the room, and marveled at the sun-streaks of blond beginning to show. Even her eyes seemed greener, brighter.

The form-hugging, green velvet gown was a perfect fit, and daringly showed off the tops of her full breasts. For the first time in her life, Jane was very pleased with what she saw in her reflection.

"What in heaven's name are you wearing!" Nelson choked out.

She plucked at the ivory lace of her demi sleeves, refusing to let him make her feel self-conscious. "The going style."

"Yes—going, going, gone! *Where* is the rest of it?"

She gave him a haughty look. "I happen to think it's lovely."

"I believe *lowly* is more the word, Miss Baker."

"Well, who cares what you think. All you ever wear is that stuffy white suit. You obviously have no taste at all in clothes."

"Where did you find that thing?"

"It belonged to Rose."

Nelson rolled his eyes. "I should have known. Miss Baker, you cannot go out there among those people looking like . . . well, like a good-time girl!"

"I certainly can't go to a formal dinner wearing a stained skirt and a dirty cotton shirt. I have to look the part," she added, adjusting her snug waist seam.

"The part of what, for heaven's sake? You are a simple, small-town librarian!"

"Not tonight. Tonight I am a high-rolling lady gambler." She picked up the silver-handled brush she'd placed on the dresser and began brushing her hair. "It wouldn't do me any good at all to look like plain Jane Baker tonight."

"I'm actually beginning to miss plain Jane Baker."

"I appreciate your concern, Nelson, but it isn't necessary. Everything is going to be just fine."

She sat down on the edge of her bed and slipped on her black loafers, which, unlike her clothes, had managed to survive the hardships of the past few days.

"*Just fine?*" Nelson retorted. "I shudder to even *think* what that means. Just how, exactly, do you plan to pull this whole charade off?"

"It's simple," Jane replied. She stood, took one last look at herself in the mirror, and reached for the door. "You're going to help me cheat."

"Of course, I—" Nelson's eyes rounded. "I'm *what?!*"

Jane tossed him a bright smile. "Gotta run."

She hurried from the stateroom before Nelson could protest her plan, and ran headlong into Dolan Kincaid. In fact, she would have stumbled over her long, heavy skirt if Dolan hadn't caught her by the shoulders and steadied her. She inhaled the fresh, musky scent he was wearing, and slowly stared up at him in absolute stunned silence.

He'd taken a bath of his own; his dark hair was still damp. He'd dressed in a crisp white shirt, black pants and jacket, and a black string tie. He'd shaved the beard stubble off his face, leaving his strong jaw smooth and revealing the sensual curve of his lips. She didn't think she'd ever seen anyone so devastatingly good-looking in all her life.

He stared down into her face with his warm blue eyes and she almost melted into her shoes. His gaze slowly traveled down her body and then back up again. "In a hurry?" he asked.

Jane had to swallow the sudden dryness in her throat before responding. "I . . . I thought I might be late," she replied.

Dolan stepped back from her, looking her over admiringly. "No, no, you're . . . right on time." He cleared his throat. "You look . . . very nice."

Jane positively beamed. She'd never looked "very nice" before. "You look very nice yourself."

"Just like the legendary Rose Diamond."

Jane's smile faltered. By his warm smile, she knew that he'd meant that as a compliment, but it hadn't felt like one to her. She hated being reminded that he still thought of her as a notorious lady outlaw.

Dolan misread her change of expression. "Don't worry," he said. "No one will suspect the very proper wife of a very proper gentleman to be a notorious lady gambler. Just watch your step, *Mrs. Kincaid.* I don't need you getting thrown overboard for cheating."

Jane blinked at him. "Thrown overboard?"

"That's what they do with cheats." He gave her a crooked smile. "So don't let them catch you."

"You *expect* me to cheat?"

"Everybody expects everybody to cheat. This isn't only a contest of who's got the best poker hand, it's a contest of who's better at palming an ace." He arched a brow at her. "You looked worried."

"I . . . I'm not. I'm just . . . not very good in crowds." Surely no one would suspect her of cheating with an angel?

He smiled broadly at her. "Just stick close to me and I'll get you through this evening."

She nodded, set her hand in the crook of his arm, and tried not to trip over her feet as he walked her down the short corridor to the main dining hall of the *Lady Gambler*.

Jane was immediately overwhelmed by the size of the crowd, and she had to fight a sudden, insane urge to throw her arms around Dolan's neck and beg him to take her away. Who was she kidding? She was never going to be able to fool all these people into believing she could play poker. They were going to find her out. They were going to uncover her little scheme and throw her overboard. Oh, why hadn't she taken swimming lessons in the third grade like all the other kids—

"Wait here while I get us something to drink," Dolan said.

He walked away, leaving her in the crowd to fend for herself, and it was all Jane could do to keep from taking off after him. A string quartet was playing Brahms in the far corner, but the music was barely heard over the din of voices in the large, packed room. She tried to steady her breathing while focusing on the elaborate crystal chandelier that was swaying gently over her head.

"Good evening."

She lowered her gaze to find a burly man standing in front of her. He smiled, crinkling his brown muttonchop whiskers, and bowed slightly to her. Jane managed a vague tremor of a smile in return. "Good evening," she replied.

"A lovely young woman such as yourself certainly has an escort this evening," the man said, his brown eyes twinkling.

"Yes, I'm . . . I'm"—she cleared her throat—"I'm here with my husband." Considering she'd just had one hell of a time choking out *that* lie, how in the world could she ever hope to pull off a larger, more elaborate fabrication, such as deceiving her way through a poker tournament?

The man placed his hand on his chest. "Ah, you've wounded my heart. The woman of my dreams is bound to another?"

She gave him an odd look. "I'm sure you'll recover."

"Only if you'll consent to taking a walk with me on deck."

He was still smiling sincerely, but Jane couldn't fathom what he possibly hoped to gain from taking a walk with her. "Why?" she blurted.

He chuckled at her question. "Because, my dear, I'd like to see if you're half so enchanting in the moonlight. I'll wager the stars cannot rival the sparkle in your magnificent eyes." He held his crooked arm out to her. "Shall we?"

Jane hesitated. Good lord, was this man hitting on her? She stared at his arm, feeling at a complete loss for words.

And then Dolan stepped up to her and thrust a fluted champagne glass into her hand. "Your drink, my love."

My love? Had everyone gone mad when she wasn't looking? Her hand shook as she took a quick, deep gulp of the golden, bubbly liquid.

Dolan turned to the man with the muttonchops, whose smile had faltered considerably. "I don't believe we've met. I'm Dolan Kincaid. And this is my wife, Jane."

Jane choked on her drink. It was the first time she'd ever heard Dolan use her real name. He clucked at her, and patted her on the back.

"Uh, the name's Beazly," the muttonchop man said. "Henry Beazly. I was just complimenting your, uh, your wife on how lovely she looks this evening."

Dolan chuckled, but the sound was decidedly chilly. "I'm sure she's heard enough of that from me tonight, Mr. Beazly. Mustn't overinflate her pretty little head, now."

The man cleared his throat. "Yes. Well. I'm off to find a table. It was a pleasure, Mrs. Kincaid, Mr. Kincaid." And Mr. Henry Beazly scampered off like a mouse evading a cat.

Jane gave Dolan a flabbergasted gape. "That man actually tried to pick me up!"

"He did *what?*" Dolan replied, his gaze hardening.

Realizing he was taking her words literally, Jane quickly rephrased herself. "I . . . I mean he made a *pass* at me. Can you even believe that?"

He gave her a bland look. "Drink your champagne."

She nodded, and downed the contents of her glass in one big gulp.

He watched her with a quizzical expression. "We'd better find a table before you fall over."

She hooked her free arm through his and he led her across the room, through various groups of chattering people, toward where the orchestra was playing. Several men turned to look at them as they strolled past. And

Jane received more than a few admiring nods, which only made her all the more nervous. Why was she attracting so much attention? It couldn't be her dress—there were certainly much more daring gowns being paraded about the floor.

"Relax," Dolan whispered close to her ear—which, of course, had the exact opposite effect on her. He tucked his arm around her waist and pulled her closer. "You're as stiff as a board."

He smiled at a passing couple, and Jane pasted on her best attempt at a smile and mimicked his performance. In the press of the crowd, she felt a sharp pinch on her backside and was glad Dolan was now holding her tightly because she truly believed she would have fallen flat on her face in that moment.

She was relieved when they finally sat down at a small booth in a corner.

"Stop smiling so much," Dolan whispered. "Your face looks like it's about to crack."

Her heart pounding in her ears, Jane relaxed her expression and handed him her tall glass. "I need another drink."

He set the glass on the white-linen-draped table in front of them. "No, you don't," he whispered. "How do you expect to play tomorrow morning with a hangover?"

That was the problem. Jane had absolutely no idea. Maybe a little liquor would lessen her inevitable humiliation?

"Relax." He slipped his arm around her waist and pulled her so close to him their thighs touched. "By lunchtime tomorrow we'll both be rich."

But Jane couldn't relax. She was realizing that she was in way over her head.

"Well, well. If it isn't the infamous lady gambler."

Dolan's expression went stone-cold, and Jane's heart nearly stopped in her chest. They both looked up at the heavyset blond man standing in front of their table and the smiling brunette clinging to his arm.

"Oh, Dicky, isn't she *lovely*," the woman said, puffing the feathers from her white boa out of her face. She was wearing a blue, beaded gown that sparkled when she moved.

The man, dressed in a black tuxedo, stuck out his broad hand. "Richard Cole."

Dolan stood, and warily took the man's hand. Jane was still holding her breath, waiting for Mr. Richard Cole to shout for security. "Dolan Kincaid," Dolan replied.

"And this is my enchanting wife, Janet," the man added. The tall, thin woman pursed her lips into a tight smile and reached out her hand to Dolan. "Charmed, I'm sure."

Then the couple turned their eyes on Jane. "I was quite surprised, as were a number of our opponents, when I learned that a woman would be playing in the tournament," Richard Cole said. "You, Mrs. Kincaid, are the talk of the room."

Mrs. Kincaid. He'd called her Mrs. Kincaid. Did that mean that he didn't think she was Rose Diamond? Jane exchanged a hopeful glance with Dolan.

Dolan gave the couple a warm smile. "My wife is an avid cardplayer."

"Yes, so I've heard," Mr. Cole replied. He laughed deeply, and patted Dolan on the shoulder. "You're quite a man, Kincaid, to indulge the little woman so shamelessly."

"Oh, Dicky," Mrs. Cole interjected, flipping the end of her boa at him. "I think it's cute. Isn't it cute?"

"Yes, dear, cute . . . very cute. Tell me, Mrs. Kincaid," he added intently, "have you ever been in one of these little competitions before?"

Jane shook her head. "As a matter of fact, no, I haven't. But—"

The man laughed, indulgently. "Well, then. You just keep your eyes on me, my dear, and I'll show you how it's done. I'll keep an eye on the little woman while she's on the floor, Kincaid."

Dolan's responding smile was chilly, to say the least. "I think my wife can hold her own just fine. I suggest you keep your eyes on your cards."

The man exchanged a raised-eyebrow look with his wife. "You sound like a gambling man yourself, Kincaid. Care to make a small wager on the game?"

"What, exactly, have you got in mind?"

"Um, darling," Jane said hesitantly. "I don't think—"

"A thousand dollars says she doesn't make it to the final round."

Dolan grunted. "That's a child's wager. A thousand dollars says she takes this tournament, lock, stock, and barrel."

Mr. Cole looked startled by the offer.

Jane tugged on Dolan's jacket. "Really, Dolan, I don't think—"

Dolan took her hand and squeezed it reassuringly. "What do you say, Cole?"

The man exchanged a broad grin with his wife, and then held his hand out to Dolan. "You've got yourself a bet, my friend."

The pair shook hands while Janet Cole looked on

with a satisfied smirk, both sides obviously thinking they'd just made an easy thousand dollars.

Jane did her best to look encouraging as Dolan smiled down at her.


The color of her dress brought out the sparkle in her eyes. Her thick blond hair, streaked pale by three days in the hot sun, fell in shimmering waves to her shoulders. She looked absolutely stunning, and Dolan couldn't take his eyes off her. Unfortunately neither could any of the other men in the room.

Her hands shook as she finished her supper of prime rib and stewed potatoes and reached for her water glass, and not for the first time Dolan wondered what was making her so nervous. They'd already put out from the dock, and were now gliding at a leisurely pace down the Sacramento River. Even if anyone did recognize her at this point, they wouldn't be able to do a damn thing about it until they docked again later the next day. And he wasn't about to let anything happen to her—now or then.

Dolan figured the chances of her being recognized were pretty damn slim anyway. This was not the cool, hard-edged, sharp-eyed Rose Diamond he had sitting at his side. No, this was a much less assured, much more refined, and very fidgety young lady. He was seriously beginning to think that Jack had been wrong about her character all along.

She leaned closer to him, inadvertently brushing the side of her breast against his arm. "That man over there keeps staring at me," she whispered. "Do you think he thinks I'm . . . I'm *her*?"

Hell, there wasn't a man in the place who wasn't staring at her, himself included. She looked amazing.

Dolan sent a scorching glance around the room until his gaze settled on the culprit. He leveled a penetrating glare on the tall, older gentleman—who promptly tugged at his necktie and averted his eyes.

"Excuse me." Dolan looked up to find another man, this one much younger, smiling down at Rose. "Have we met?" the young man asked.

Dolan sighed impatiently as Rose gave him a frantic look. "My wife has only just arrived in America after an extensive trip abroad," he replied coolly. If the young pup didn't stop grinning down at her like a hungry wolf he was going to tear the smirk right off his damn face.

"Your wife?" the man repeated, still smiling.

"That's right," Dolan responded. "My *wife*."

"You're a very lucky man."

*And you're going to be a very dead one if you don't move the hell on,* Dolan thought icily. He smiled tightly. "Thank you."

The man reluctantly wandered off, and Dolan settled a cold stare on the far wall. He was actually feeling jealous. He couldn't believe it. After all the trouble he'd gone to to deny his attraction to Rose Diamond, she'd still managed to get under his skin.

She leaned toward him again. "Why are you scowling?" she asked softly.

He grunted, thinking that if she brushed herself up against his arm one more time he wasn't going to be responsible for his actions. "I didn't know I was."

"It makes me nervous when you scowl. It makes me think something's gone wrong."

He sighed and looked into her eyes while mentally

reaching out and running his fingers along the silky nape of her neck. "Nothing can go wrong. I've now got *three* thousand dollars riding on you."

Her gaze held his for a lingering moment before they were interrupted.

"Ah, there you are, Mr. Kincaid."

Johnathon McIntire, the owner of the *Lady Gambler,* paused at their table and Dolan stood for the introductions. "Mr. McIntire. May I introduce my wife Jane."

The tall, distinguished man bestowed a broad, bright smile on Rose Diamond, and took her small hand in his. "Mrs. Kincaid. I'm very pleased to meet you. Your husband tells me that you will be playing in the tournament tomorrow morning."

She cleared her throat delicately. "Yes," she answered with a tremulous smile.

"Tell me, is poker in England all that much different than poker in the States?"

She blinked, obviously taken off guard by the question, and Dolan quickly jumped in. "You don't expect my wife to tell you all her secrets now, do you, Mr. McIntire?"

The man chuckled. "Of course not. Mrs. Kincaid, I hope to see you sitting at the finalists' table tomorrow."

She stared openly after the man as he walked away, and Dolan felt something bitter settle heavily into his stomach as he sat back down beside her. "If you're finished gawking at our host, maybe you'd like me to point out a few of your other opponents for tomorrow's game?"

She turned back to him. And she was smiling. Something deep inside of Dolan melted in that moment, and he knew he was in deep, deep trouble. "These men are actually flirting with me," she said, looking bemused.

She had the expression of a child who'd just discovered candy. "And why wouldn't they?" he replied. "You're the most beautiful woman in the room."

She gave him a startled look, and then a blush slowly crept into her cheeks.

"Now pay attention. You see that man over there in the scarlet vest?"

She followed the direction of his nod.

"That's Will Baits. He's from Nevada. His daddy's loaded with cash, and ol' Will's got a reputation for joining up with these tourneys just for something to do. Don't let whatever flashy clothes he wears tomorrow intimidate you. Now that fellow over there . . . "

Again she followed his nod.

". . . that's Three Finger Jake. Ever heard of him?"

She shook her head.

"Don't let his missing digits fool you into thinking he can't play cards. Jake is reputed to be one of the connivingest cardsharps west of the Rockies."

She nodded, and pointed to a man wearing a lime-green jacket, dull yellow pants, and a flashy redhead on his arm. "Who's that man?"

"That's Pete Paulson. He was the big winner last year. He's the one to beat. He has a reputation for going for the flush."

She gave him a hesitant look, as if she had no idea what he was talking about.

Dolan couldn't tell whether she was too nervous to hear him right, or just playing with his mind again. The way things had been progressing all evening, he figured it could be either and/or both. "Flush, Miss— *Jane.*

Paulson goes for the flush. Are you feeling all right—you're looking a little pale."

"I'm a little tired. How much longer do we need to stay?"

Frankly, Dolan would be happy to get her out of that room and away from all those searching male glances. He stood, and offered her his hand. "I think we've put in a good enough appearance."

All eyes were on them as they left the dining hall—all eyes were on his beautiful companion, anyway.

Dolan led her down the long hallway toward the number three stateroom and used his key to unlock the door. She turned toward him on the threshold. "Thank you for a lovely evening."

A man could drown in those liquid green eyes, he warned himself. "You're welcome," he replied, and attempted to brush past her for entrance into the room.

She sidestepped and blocked his way. "Um, I'm really tired," she said with a faint laugh. "And if you want me to do my best tomorrow, I'm going to need all the rest I can get."

He nodded. "Fine." And then he tried to walk by her again.

Again she stepped into his path. "Mr. Kincaid, I really would like to go to bed."

"I understand."

She paused, expectantly. "And I'd really like it if you would retire to your own room."

Ah. Now Dolan understood. In all the excitement he'd forgotten to inform her of the sleeping arrangements.

He pushed past her into the stateroom and closed the door behind him. "Why, Mrs. Kincaid," he said, grinning, "this *is* my own room."

# 12

*Jane lay in her bed late that night,* staring silently up at the molded tin of her stateroom ceiling. She was frustrated and restless. She had things to do—certain angels to contact—in order to prepare for the next morning. The only game of cards she'd ever played was Go Fish, and she highly doubted that that was anything remotely comparable to Five Card Stud. Nelson was her only hope of sparing Dolan the loss of three thousand dollars.

But Dolan had had the audacity to assign them both to the same room.

Dolan's excuse was that he wanted to keep up their appearance of being man and wife. But Jane suspected their sharing had more to do with the fact that he didn't trust her enough to leave her alone for the night, a suspicion punctuated by the gun that he had tucked beneath his pillow.

How could he want to kiss her one moment, and not trust her out of his sight the very next?

Now her only hope of contacting Nelson was if she could manage to sneak out of the room.

She glanced at the alarm clock on the bed, the one Dolan had set for seven o'clock the next morning. It was half past one. She was running out of time.

She listened carefully to his deep, even breathing for a moment, and then slowly, soundlessly, slipped to the edge of her bed. The moonlight coming in from the casement window cast a silver glow throughout the room and down upon the floor where Dolan was sleeping. Even in the pale moonlight, he was the handsomest man Jane had ever seen.

She unwrapped her voluminous nightgown from around her legs—something else she'd found tucked down in her great-aunt Rosanna's saddlebags—and with careful, slow movements stepped down onto the narrow floor space between Dolan and the bed. She stepped over him, straddling him, and he stirred. She froze stiffer than a pine tree, and remained there, immobile, for what seemed like hours, until his breathing once again turned deep and rhythmic.

At that point, Jane finally eked out the breath she'd been holding. She could only imagine the conclusions Dolan would jump to if he woke and found her sneaking from the—

"Where the hell do you think you're going?"

He startled her so badly she nearly jumped out of her skin. She glared down at him furiously. "For a walk." She moved to step over him.

He grabbed her bare ankle in a warm, tight grip that sent a burst of tingles shooting up her calf. "You can walk tomorrow."

"Mr. Kincaid," Jane said, staring down at him. "You have no right to keep me here."

"I bought myself two thousand dollars' worth of rights, lady."

Jane gritted her teeth, and tried to wrench her leg from his grasp. "I need some fresh air."

"Then open the goddamn window."

"I have to go to the bathroom," she said tightly.

"Then open the goddamn window," he reiterated.

"You are absolutely impossible!"

"I like to think so. Now get your butt back in that bed before I toss you there myself."

She turned, and lunged back onto the feather mattress. "I feel like I'm in jail all over again!" she stated bitterly, while yanking the blankets over her and flopping onto her back.

"Just relax and concentrate on winning tomorrow."

"And what if I don't win?" she retorted. "What if the other players are just plain better than I am?"

"Don't get cold feet on me now, Miss Diamond. I've been waiting for this opportunity for three long years."

Damn. There came those cold, niggling feelings of guilt again. The ones that made Jane feel as if she were literally snatching money right out of the man's hands. She rolled her eyes and stared at the ceiling once again. "How can you risk so much money on a person you don't even trust enough to let go to the bathroom alone?"

"I trust in your pride enough to know that once you're seated at the poker table you won't throw the game just to spite me."

"But what if I don't win?" she insisted. She rolled to the side of the bed and looked down on him. "What if I try my best and still lose?"

"Rose Diamond never loses."

Jane slammed her hands down onto the mattress. "*Jane*, damn it! My name is Jane!"

He sat up and gave her an intense look. "Move over."

She scowled at him as he rose to his feet. "What? Why?"

"Because you never seem to give up, lady. And I'm not about to sleep with one eye open all night making sure you don't sneak out of the room."

Jane was flabbergasted. "You're not sleeping with me!"

"That is exactly what I'm doing." He sat down on the edge of the mattress, giving Jane little choice but to scoot over or be sat upon.

"What in God's name is this going to solve?" she demanded.

He sighed, lifted his stockinged feet, and stretched out beside her on the narrow bed. "It's going to stop you from sneaking off for some shameless liaison and blowing our happy husband and wife disguise to the moon."

"*Shameless liaison?*" Jane replied incredulously.

"What other reason could you have for trying to sneak out in the middle of the night? Unless, of course, you plan to jump overboard and swim a mile to shore."

"If you must know, I was going to talk with Nelson," she retorted, not caring at this point what he would think of her. "He's going to help me win tomorrow."

"Uh huh. Send him a prayer instead." He rolled toward her and threw his heavy leg over hers.

"What are you doing now?" she cried, suddenly finding herself pinned to the mattress.

"Keeping you from slinking off while I'm asleep."

"Mr. Kincaid, this is— This is ludicrous!" Not to mention just a bit overwhelming. Jane was suddenly finding it very difficult to breathe.

"Would you prefer rope?"

Now that he mentioned it—yes! "Why can't you just accept my word that I won't run—"

"Shhhh. I'm trying to sleep."

"But I—"

"Shhhh," he said, curling against her side.

Jane went perfectly still, afraid to twitch even the slightest muscle. But she couldn't control her breathing, which quickly became erratic, or her mind, which began racing wildly, or her heart rate, which went from fifty to one hundred in three point five seconds.

And that was how she lay there, mentally and physically frantic, for close to ten minutes as Dolan Kincaid's breathing slowly turned rhythmic and steady. Now she had two strong reasons for wanting to escape the stateroom: Nelson, and the attractive man lying next to her.

Time slowly ticked past. Dolan's body grew warm and comfortable beside her. And Jane gradually began to relax. She found herself trying to match the sound of his breathing, but then settle into a rhythm all her own as her mind began to drift.

But then every nerve ending in her body suddenly came alive as Dolan snuggled his face against the side of her neck.

Jane's breathing all but stopped. "M-Mr. Kincaid?" she whispered.

He groaned in his sleep, his warm breath tickling her ear, and her eyes flew open wide as his arm flopped over her stomach. He mumbled something unintelligible and pulled her tightly against his hard body, while Jane barely held in a screech of alarm.

But when his hot lips brushed over the sensitive skin of her neck, she squeezed her eyes shut and did battle with a totally insane urge to encourage him.

\*          \*          \*

Okay, so pretending he was asleep was a pretty cowardly way to come on to a lady.

But Dolan didn't know how else to make an advance to this completely attractive, totally perplexing woman. He was afraid that if he made an obvious pass, she'd either faint in his arms or sock him right between the eyes.

He was so incredibly aroused by her warmth and her softness. For three straight days he'd fought his attraction, telling himself he'd be nuts to let himself fall for a notorious outlaw like Rose Diamond. But, with still no sign of the heartless woman Jack had warned him about, Dolan was finding the gentle, resourceful woman he'd come to know harder and harder to resist.

She smelled like roses after a warm rain. Her skin was as soft and dewy as a petal. The long, wide nightgown she had on wasn't exactly revealing, but that only made Dolan's imagination fill in the missing pieces, made him wonder just what she might look like beneath all those yards of white cotton.

She was as stiff as a board in his arms, telling him in no uncertain terms that she wasn't going to be receptive to his advances—sleep-induced or otherwise. So he decided he'd settle for a kiss. One simple kiss. Well, as simple as one of their kisses could be, anyway; the heat they seemed to generate whenever their lips touched was damn near combustible.

With a precision born of years of practice, he moved his hand up her stomach, between her breasts, which were very hard to pass up, and to her delicate jaw, where he subtly turned her face toward him.

He nuzzled her cheek, feeling the silky texture of her skin with his lips. He kissed her chin, tasting the dainty curve with the tip of his tongue. And then his mouth found hers in the moonlight.

The first tentative touch of their lips made her jolt in his arms, but Dolan wasn't about to be deterred. He whispered gently to her, and urged her to turn toward him. He kissed her again, carefully, and then took sweet, full possession of her mouth, determined to once and for all uncover the truth behind these powerful feelings he had for her.

Half of him expected her to fight him. But she didn't. The other half expected her to turn into the seductive temptress he'd heard so much about and take over completely. But she didn't do that either. What she did was kiss him back, sweetly, tenderly, with an innocence that almost undid him. He gently parted her lips with his tongue and deepened their embrace. She let out a tiny moan in response, and slipped her arms around his neck. He almost came out of his skin as she arched her back and curved her lush body against his.

He cupped the high, round curves of her bottom. This woman was a perfect fit in his arms. It was almost as if she were carved right out of him. He pressed her hips forward against the hard length of him beneath the denims he'd kept on, and she didn't pull away. In fact, the way she was clinging to him, the way she was kissing him, led him to believe that she wanted to give him more.

"Ah, Jesus, Rose," he whispered against her soft lips. All of a sudden she lurched away from him as if he were on fire—which he damn near was. She sat up in the bed, and he looked at her in surprise, the taste of her still on his lips. She stared down at him with shadowed eyes.

She was breathing fast, and even in the faint moonlight he could see that she was flushed with desire.

He sat up beside her. "What is it?"

Tears were filling her eyes, and he felt a strong pang of guilt stab at his heart. He'd obviously moved too fast for her. "I'm . . . I'm sorry."

"For what?" she asked, her voice raw with emotion.

"For . . . pressuring you," he replied.

"For pressuring who?" she asked, her voice rising a bit.

He gave her an odd look, one tainted with sexual frustration. "Well, that's a pretty absurd question."

"I think it's a very legitimate question, Mr. Kincaid. *Who*, exactly, were you kissing just now?"

"Oh, for Christ's sake," he snapped. "You—the infamous Rose Diamond."

Her expression hardened, and she opened her mouth as if she were about to verbally lambaste him. But then her expression changed, to one of hopelessness, and she closed her eyes and slowly lay back down on the bed.

"What the hell did I do?" he cried.

"I know this bed is small, but I would appreciate it if you'd stay on your side of it. Good night."

Quietly astounded, Dolan stared down at her expectantly, not willing to believe that she would end their passionate encounter without telling him what the hell had gone wrong. Didn't their kisses affect her as much as they did him? If not, why did she kiss him back with all the passion he was feeling? *Why the hell had she pulled away from him?*

Intending to ask her just that, he leaned toward her. But the deep, even sound of her breathing made him hesitate. He knew she was tired. And she certainly needed her rest for tomorrow.

He flopped onto his back, and stared up at the ceiling in the moonlight. His body was aching for hers.

Finally, after a few minutes of silence, he knew he couldn't stand going through the night like this. He rolled toward her, intending to wake her the hell up and make her tell him what the hell had gone wrong between them. But he stopped short at the sight she presented, a sight that made him prop his head in his hand and stare at her; watch the smooth rise and fall of her chest, the faint flutter of her eyelashes against her cheeks, the gentle parting of her full lips as she breathed. Her hair was fanned out in a dark gold cloud against the stark white of the pillow slip, and he reached out and carefully tucked a silken strand away from her face.

How could a woman who seemed so much like an angel be the devil in disguise? He couldn't imagine her swatting a fly, let alone shooting a man in a dark alleyway.

She sighed, and turned her head away from him, and he reluctantly lay back down on his pillow. It was probably for the best that she'd ended their embrace. A woman like Rose Diamond had no place in the quiet, respectable life he had planned for himself.

Tomorrow she'd win that tournament. And then he'd let her go.

The idea of that struck Dolan hard in the stomach. He'd only known her three days, and he'd already grown used to having her underfoot.

But he'd keep his promise. He'd hand over her share of the winnings once he'd escorted her safely out of Sacramento. And then he'd try not to linger over what-ifs and might-have-beens as he rode north and she headed off in the opposite direction.

# 13

*Jane stood in a deserted corner* on deck with the morning sun at her back. She was trying to look inconspicuous—a hard thing to do while calling for an angel.

She'd chosen a secluded spot just beneath one of the tall, black smokestacks of the paddle wheeler, hoping it would be an unpopular place for the other passengers, but people were still milling past every now and then, giving her odd glances. Hopefully people weren't tossed overboard for being lunatics as well as cheats.

She felt tired and emotionally exhausted after another restless night with Dolan Kincaid by her side. But she was no less determined to win that poker tournament for him. It was bad enough that she was deceiving him by the mere acceptance of his deal; she wasn't going to lose all his money on top of that.

But the players were expected at their assigned tables in less than thirty minutes, and Jane's secret weapon was nowhere to be found.

"Nelson!" she called for probably the twentieth time in as many minutes. "Appear, damn it!"

"Miss Baker, I find your new habit of cursing extremely distressing. A habit picked up from that bounty hunter, no doubt."

She sighed with relief as Nelson materialized, sitting on the mahogany railing a few feet away. "Well, it's about time," she said, moving toward him. "The game is scheduled to start in less than a half an hour."

"Really," he said blandly. "How nice."

"Nelson," she said impatiently, "we need to plan a strategy."

"*We?*" he questioned, arching his pale brows. "Do you perhaps have a small rodent in the pocket of that ridiculous dress?"

Jane frowned down at her yellow gingham dress. It was short-sleeved and high-waisted, and had a square neckline that made her neck look long and graceful. She found she had quite an appreciation for her great-aunt's taste in clothes. "I think it's very flattering."

"Where ever did you get it? Chez Little House on the Prairie?"

"Don't change the subject, Nelson. We haven't got the time. Now, I was thinking—"

He laughed. "Oh, Miss Baker, *I* have all the time in the world."

Jane stared at him, and then pursed her lips with a frosty glare. "You aren't going to help me, are you."

"Angels, my dear, do not cheat at cards—nor do they instruct others on the art of doing so."

"No, they just flit around trying to kill their clients," she snapped.

He gave her a dark scowl. "What I am going to say next comes from the deepest recesses of my heart, and is said with all the best intentions: Leap over this railing, woman, and drown like a dog! Do it, and this entire *absurd* situation will be over and done with once and for all!"

Jane crossed her arms over her chest. "I promised Dolan I would play, and I am *going* to play. Whether you help me or not."

"I swear you are the most *exasperating* woman I have ever met. And to think that for one moment I actually thought you retiring and compliant. There's a tempest lurking around in that soul of yours, Miss Baker. A *tempest*!"

Jane broke into a proud grin. "Why, thank you, Nelson. I think that's the nicest thing anyone's ever said to me." She turned her smile on an older couple who were staring oddly at her as they passed. "Now. Are you going to help me or not?"

"I have been *trying* to help you all along!"

"I need you to help me play poker, Nelson. Not help me off a cliff."

"Miss Baker, even if I wanted to help you, the art of card-playing cannot be *crammed* into a lesson of not even thirty minutes."

"Which is why I'm going to need you at the table with me."

Nelson sighed, and then he narrowed his eyes on her. "And what exactly might you be willing to give me in return for my help?"

"What do you mean?"

"I'm willing to make a deal with you, Miss Baker."

Jane rolled her eyes. "Great. Another deal."

"I'll help you any way I can during this poker tournament, if you will promise me that when the time comes you will willingly return to the twentieth century, where you belong."

Jane gave him a strange smile. "Why in heaven's name wouldn't I?"

"Promise me."

She shrugged. "No problem. I promise."

"All right then. Let's begin—"

A tingle of excitement raced through Jane. "Oh, this is going to be so exciting."

"Excitement, my dear, is in the eye of the beholder, and we both know that you've been a bit nearsighted for years."

"Nelson, I have spent my whole life hiding behind the safety of monotony, running from the slightest challenge. This is my big chance to prove to myself that I'm capable of more than just stamping library cards. I'm finally going to live!"

The angel's expression softened a bit. "You have come a very long way in just a few short days, Miss Baker. You should be very proud of yourself."

"You know what, Nelson? I am."

"And I suppose you feel a bit of gratitude toward Mr. Kincaid for some of your newfound confidence."

Suddenly that kiss, that incredible, nerve-tingling embrace that she and Dolan had shared the night before, came surging to the forefront of Jane's mind. She'd never experienced anything like that kiss, never even let herself believe that a simple touching of lips could be so electrifying. She'd melted in his arms, lost herself in his embrace. Prepared to give up her heart, body, and soul to him.

And then he'd called her Rose.

All the taunts and slurs she'd heard her whole life combined couldn't have hurt her more.

She smiled at Nelson, hoping her expression looked convincing. "I suppose I am."

"Miss Baker," Nelson said with an assessing gaze, "are you in love with the man?"

Jane blinked at him in surprise. She supposed she did feel something for Dolan. But love? Could that be what made her heart pound whenever he stood near, what made her palms sweaty whenever he smiled, what sent her senses reeling every time he kissed her?

Regardless, her feelings certainly weren't reciprocated. There was no way in the world an exciting man like Dolan Kincaid could be interested in a plain-Jane woman like herself.

"Miss Baker?"

She recovered from her thoughts and gave Nelson another weak smile. "Of course not," she replied. But even as she denied it, a part of her knew she was lying.

Dolan sat at the long mahogany bar amid a horde of other spectators as the ten contestants in the Sacramento Poker Tournament took their seats at their assigned game tables. His "wife," the lovely Mrs. Jane Kincaid, was seated at the center table with Pete Paulson, a gentleman by the name of Guy Stanley, and a bear of a man named Jacob Brown. She was the only woman of the sixteen players entered in the tournament, and she looked like a rare wildflower in the midst of a bunch of scraggly weeds.

Dolan had finally managed to fall asleep just as dawn was brightening their stateroom, and at that point he'd slept so heavily that he hadn't heard Rose rise and go up on deck. But that was where he'd found her five minutes ago, leaning against the railing, staring out at the sparkling river.

She was beautiful, magical. He could sense her nervousness about the game, and wanted to take her into his arms and reassure her that everything was going to be fine. But her rejection of him the night before was still raw in his mind, and his pride wasn't about to let him take any more risks where she was concerned.

He'd escorted her off the deck and into the main hall, where he'd helped her find her seat. Now all that was left for him to do was sit back, watch, and wait.

Play began promptly at 8 A.M., and he could tell by the way her hands shook when she picked up her first hand of cards that Rose was as nervous as hell. She was actually making *him* feel a little jittery, and he had to remind himself that this was the woman who'd bested every cardplayer south of San Francisco.

But as the first bets were placed, Dolan found himself sweating. What if she didn't win? He didn't have just three thousand dollars riding on this game; he had his entire future. And could the notorious Rose Diamond handle losing?

Knowing the first round could wind on for hours, he turned to the bartender and ordered a whiskey straight up. Then he keyed in on a conversation taking place beside him between three men looking over a day-old copy of the *Sacramento Bee*.

"Happened yesterday at dawn," a man in a black jacket was saying.

His friend smiled through his thick brown beard. "Now that's swift justice."

"A waste of good female flesh, if you ask me," the third, balding man replied, and tossed back his drink. The other two broke into agreeable laughter.

And then the bearded man noticed Dolan's interest and smiled at him. "You hear the news, friend?"

Dolan's drink was set on the counter before him and he took a sip. "What news is that?"

The man in the black jacket handed him the paper. "The news about Rose Diamond."

Dolan's fingers dug into the folded newspaper as every muscle in his body went string-tight. "What about her?"

The bearded man slid his empty glass toward the bartender for a refill. "She was hanged yesterday morning."

Dolan didn't say a word while he waited for the man's shaggy face to break out in a joking grin. But not a single whisker on that hairy face so much as twitched. "And where did you hear that?" he finally asked, as calmly as he could manage.

The bald man nodded toward the paper in Dolan's hands. "Read for yourself."

Dolan slowly opened the paper and stared in stupefaction at the headline on the front page. "Barkeep," he said hoarsely, "another whiskey."

NOTORIOUS MURDERESS HANGED BY THE NECK UNTIL DEAD, it read.

And just below that was an article that began with her name in big bold type:

> **Rose Diamond**, infamous cardsharp, was found
> guilty of the crime of murder yesterday evening
> in a court of law governed by Judge Hugh
> Colfax. In accordance with California law she
> was thereby sentenced to death by hanging, and
> was given swift justice this morning at sunrise
> before a crowd of over two hundred.

The article went on to describe the event, but Dolan's mind wandered at that point. *Dead? Rose Diamond was dead?*

He slowly, dazedly, laid the paper on the bar.

"You okay, friend?" the balding man asked.

"You know the lady?" the bearded one inquired. Dolan ignored them both as he turned toward the main floor and settled his gaze on the woman he'd been with for four days. She was in the process of looking over her cards. His gaze traveled over her golden fall of hair, the smooth cast of her profile, the slight curve at the corner of her mouth as she concentrated.

She was gentle. Graceful. Delicate—everything Rose Diamond was reputed not to be. How in God's name could he have been so blind? She'd been telling him all along that her name was Jane. Jane Baker. A simple name for a simple woman. But he'd been too stubborn, too bent on winning this tournament to pay any attention to her claims.

And maybe there was a small part of him that hadn't wanted to believe her, knowing that if she wasn't really Rose Diamond, then he'd have to let her go.

She wasn't Rose. Dear God, he couldn't believe it. She wasn't Rose Diamond! She wasn't scheming and vicious, heartless and unconscionable. She wasn't a thief, or a murderer. Hell, she probably really *didn't* know how to play poker—

Dolan's eyes flew wide, and he lunged up from the bar stool. Holy shit! He'd just thrown three thousand dollars right out the goddamn window!

He was down the four steps and onto the main floor before his heart even had a chance to start pumping again. He was five feet from Jane Baker, and still trying to figure out just exactly what he intended to do when he reached her, when his arm was grasped firmly by one of McIntire's armed guards. "I'm sorry, sir, but you'll have to stay off the main floor until the first round is over."

Dolan stared at the large man, tempted to punch him right in the nose and take his chances. But it didn't matter if he picked up Miss Jane Baker and removed her bodily from the game. His two-thousand-dollar stake was nonrefundable. He couldn't get it back. And he doubted Richard Cole would care to hear the sad story of his foolishness.

She gave him a bewildered look as he was escorted back to the steps leading to the bar. Dolan didn't know whether to be enraged with himself or with her. She'd certainly tried to warn him enough times. And he was sure she'd felt that if *he* believed her to be Rose Diamond, the judge and jury in Sacramento would believe the exact same thing. He'd left her with little choice but to agree to his deal—which had been nothing short of blackmail.

He'd created this mess with his own stubbornness. And he was about to pay for it in spades.


"Stop gawking at Mr. Kincaid and pay attention to the game, Miss Baker."

Jane gave Nelson a sharp glance. He was standing behind Mr. Paulson, who was champing down on a short, fat cigar. She wasn't sure why Dolan had come storming down from the bar, but that stunned expression on his face had sent a chill down her spine. Something was definitely wrong.

Suddenly a man at the table next to hers was yanked up from his seat by one of the large guards. His coat lapels were jerked aside and two aces of spades fluttered to the floor. The other men at his table shouted encouragement as the cheater was taken by the back of his jacket, led out of the main hall, and unceremoniously tossed overboard to swim back to shore on his own.

A fine sheen of sweat broke out on Jane's brow.

"Don't fret, Miss Baker," Nelson said from behind her. "I highly doubt they'll suspect you're winning by means of heavenly intervention. Now, ask for two cards and lay down your four and ten of hearts."

Jane did as she was told, having absolutely no idea what she was doing. She was dealt two more cards and situated them in her hand.

"No, no, don't arrange them. You're only signaling to the others that they fit somewhere in your hand. Arrange them in your mind, Miss Baker, in your *mind*." Flustered, Jane stopped arranging her cards and stared instead at the pile of colorful wooden chips in the center of the table.

"Call," Nelson told her.

"What?" she whispered.

The others at the table glanced up at her and she broke into a hesitant smile.

"The bid is yours, Mrs. Kincaid," Mr. Stanley said, "at one hundred dollars."

"*Call*," Nelson repeated firmly.

"How?" Jane whispered through her smile.

"Oh for heaven's sake, just toss in one of those little yellow chips and say 'call'!"

Jane quickly did just that, and was relieved when the

table's attention was then directed at the man sitting beside her.

Nelson was mopping his brow with a white silk hanky. "Good heavens, Miss Baker, if we pull this off it will be a miracle indeed."

One by one the men laid their hands faceup on the table. Until they were all once again staring at her. "Mrs. Kincaid?" Mr. Brown prompted.

"Hmm?"

"Your hand?"

"Oh." With a shaking fingers, Jane laid her cards out on the table and watched the other three men sigh in resignation.

"What?" she said, alarmed. "Did I do something wrong?"

Mr. Stanley smiled painfully. "Not if you call winning wrong, Mrs. Kincaid. Your three kings beat anything we've got."

Jane blinked in astonishment. "I . . . I win? I mean—" She cleared her throat and repeated more firmly, "I win."

"Retrieve your pot, Miss Baker," Nelson said dryly, "before they decide you're too ridiculous to claim it."

Jane quickly reached out and scooped all the various colored chips toward her. "Can they do that?" she asked softly.

"In your case," Nelson muttered, "I think they might just make an exception."

Another round was dealt out, and Jane won that one as well. The next, however, she folded on, at Nelson's command, and was glad for it when Mr. Brown laid down a hand of hearts with the numbers all in a row. Nelson informed her that that was called a straight flush, a practically unbeatable hand—and one that she should aspire to get for herself.

The game played on for hours, as did the string quartet in the background. Jane won the majority of hands, eagerly stacking her chips in her rack at the end of each round. She was really beginning to get the hang of things. However, the others at the table seemed to not only be growing a bit irritated by her constant wins, they also seemed to be growing a bit suspicious.

They all began watching her closely, and Nelson warned her not to place her free hand in her lap unless she wanted to be charged with palming cards.

One by one her four opponents were drained of their poker chips, until it was just Jane and Mr. Brown seated at the table. By this time they'd been playing for four hours. And Jane wasn't the least bit tired. She'd become completely entrenched in the game.

The round went first to Mr. Brown, and then to Jane. Back and forth they went, until the crowd started to grow weary, and spectators started to fall asleep in their seats. The other three tables had decided their finalists. All that was left was for either Jane or Mr. Brown to finish the other off.

Jane stared at her hand. It looked as if this would be Mr. Brown's round. She was holding the three of spades, the six of spades, the seven of spades, the queen of spades, and the king of diamonds: the type of hand Nelson liked to call scattered rubbish.

She unfanned her hand and prepared to fold.

"Ask for one card."

She gave Nelson a startled look.

"Don't gape at me like a blasted bunny caught in headlights; ask for one card."

Jane refanned her hand, and stared at her cards, trying to see what Nelson obviously saw: some sort of value to what she was holding. She saw nothing but a bunch of useless numbers—none of them matching or in any order. She looked up at the dealer, hoping Nelson knew what he was doing, and cleared her throat. "One, please."

The dealer slid her one card.

"Give him back the king," Nelson said.

Perplexed even more, Jane slid the highest card in her hand toward the dealer, and then picked up the king of spades. Her heart sank. She'd traded in a king for a king. Mr. Brown started the bidding, tossing out two one-hundred-dollar chips. He was obviously very confident in his hand.

Jane looked at Nelson, who was standing behind Mr. Brown. "Bet everything you have against everything he has," he said.

She froze. Nelson had obviously lost his mind. She certainly wasn't going to bet everything she had on this nothing little hand.

"Just do it, Miss Baker," Nelson said with an irritable sigh.

Jane took a deep breath and pushed her entire tray of chips toward the center of the table. "I'll . . . I'll bet everything I have against . . . against everything you have," she announced with a show of confidence she didn't quite feel.

The room broke out in a gasp, and people were startled from their dozes. Mr. Brown gave Jane a surprised look. And then he broke into a catlike smile around the thick stub of his cigar. "Well, all right, little lady," he said. "I suppose this has gone on long enough." He pushed his own tray of chips into the center of the table. Then he laid down his hand. He had a straight to the queen. Five little cards all in a row.

Jane's heart dropped. She gave Nelson a stunned glare. He'd ruined her! He'd made her bet everything she had on scattered rubbish! With a firm set to her jaw, and tears springing to her eyes, she slowly laid down her hand.

Another gasp went up from the crowd and Jane felt totally humiliated. What kind of idiot bet everything she had on . . . on . . .

"Mrs. Kincaid wins with a flush," the dealer announced.

Jane stared at the mustached man in shock. She looked down at her hand.

"All spades, Miss Baker," Nelson said. "Formally called a flush."

Jane broke into a smile as the crowd began to applaud.

"I warned you that poker could not be learned in thirty minutes," Nelson told her. "And I certainly wasn't going to stand around all day while you traded pots back and forth with Mr. Cigar, here."

"Thank you, Nelson," she said as the crowd surged noisily around her. "Thank you!"

"Thank me when it's all over, Miss Baker. The final is yet to come."

With that, the angel faded away and Jane was swept up in the revelry. She couldn't believe it. She'd actually made it to the final round. Dolan had to be thrilled—

A steely hand clamped down on her arm, and she was swung around and brought up hard against Dolan's broad chest. "Congratulations," he said.

She heedlessly threw her arms around his neck as the

crowd jostled around them. "I did it, Dolan!" she cried. "I did it!"

"Ladies and gentlemen," Johnathon McIntire called from the steps leading down out to the main deck. "We have our four finalists. The first is Mr. Jake Haskell of Turlock, Montana. The second is Mr. Stan Lister of Silver Springs, Nevada. The third is Mr. Richard Cole of San Francisco, and"—he turned a broad smile on Jane—"the fourth is the lovely Mrs. Dolan Kincaid of Littleville, California." He paused until the crowd had finished their applause. "Play shall resume in exactly"—he checked his pocket watch—"two hours from now. I suggest our players get some rest. Good luck to each and every one of you."

Jane smiled at numerous offers of congratulations. And then tensed as Mr. Richard Cole strode up to them with his wife on his arm. Her boa was pink today.

"Well," Mr. Cole said. "It looks as if the lady had quite a stroke of luck this morning."

"If luck is what it can be called," his smirking wife added suggestively.

"Well, I—"

"My wife needs her rest," Dolan interrupted. Grateful for the reprieve, Jane followed along behind Dolan as he led her from the room. He practically dragged her down the hallway and into their stateroom, where he shut the door tightly behind them.

Jane turned to him, almost bursting with excitement. "Dolan, I won!" she cried. "I can't believe it!"

"Congratulations."

She frowned playfully at him. "Well, I thought you'd be a little more excited than this."

"I probably would be if things were more like they

seemed. But we both know they're not. Don't we."

She blinked at him. "What are you talking about?" She laughed. "I *won*!"

"I'm talking about this."

He held a newspaper up in front of her nose, and Jane stared at it in confusion. But as she slowly read the front-page headline, all the blood drained from her face and dropped down to her toes.

Rose Diamond was dead.

# 14

*In shock,* Jane gaped at the headline. Rose Diamond had been hanged. And Dolan Kincaid was now looking as if he planned to make it a double funeral.

He dangled the newspaper in front of her face. "Apparently, you were tried two days ago, *Rose.* And hanged yesterday at dawn," he finished angrily.

"I told you I wasn't Rose Diamond!" she shouted in defense. "I told you over and *over* again! It's not my fault that you're so damn pigheaded!"

He threw the newspaper to the floor. "The two of you were in cahoots, weren't you? You and Rose. What are you, twins or something?"

"Oh, come on. Can't you just *accept* that you made a mistake? It happens to the best of us, Mr. Kincaid."

"You were her red herring, giving her the time and opportunity to get away from me."

Jane gritted her teeth. "You are the most narrow-minded, stubborn man—"

Dolan took her by the shoulders. "I've wasted my

time, my energy—and blown three goddamn thousand dollars on you, lady!"

"*I won!*" Jane shouted up into his face. "Or didn't you hear all the applause?!"

"Of course I heard it. I've been glued to the edge of a goddamn bar stool all morning! You were *lucky*! I don't know how you did it, but anyone who cheats as much as you must have is bound to get caught eventually. And now you're going to be up against the three best players in the whole goddamn room." He released her and rubbed his forehead in frustration. "Christ, we may as well jump overboard right now."

"Unfortunately I can't swim," Jane said dryly, straightening the neckline of her dress.

"Christ," he muttered tightly. "I can't believe this."

"Mr. Kincaid, no one is going to catch me cheating."

"Nobody can cheat on every hand and not get caught eventually. Not even Rose Diamond."

"I can. I did." She gave him a confident smile. "And I will."

His glare deepened.

"Nelson is helping me."

Dolan threw his hands up in the air. "Good Christ! If you're trying to reassure me, you're failing miserably!"

"He happens to be a very good cardplayer," Jane pressed on. "And he's assuring my wins by keeping an eye on the other players' hands."

"Look, I understand why you felt the need to act like a lunatic before I knew the whole truth. God knows I would have tried anything to get out of hanging for somebody else's crimes. But the scheming is over now. Finished. Christ, the whole damn thing's finished."

"I can still win," Jane insisted. "That money is as good as yours."

He laughed bitterly. "You and Rose have gotta be related. Neither one of you knows when to give the hell up!"

"Maybe we just aren't as anxious to quit as you are!" she retorted.

He narrowed his eyes and considered her carefully. "Just who the hell are you?"

Jane sighed. "I told you. I'm Jane—"

"Baker. A librarian. One who can dodge bullets, chase off Indians, and cheat at poker like a son of a bitch."

He took her by the arm and pulled her close. Surprise made Jane brace her hands against his hard chest as his blue eyes burned down into hers and searched her face. "How could I have been so blind?" he muttered.

"I . . . I didn't mean to mislead you," she answered, trying not to grow frightened by his sudden intensity.

"The tattoo should have tipped me off."

"T-tattoo?"

"Rose Diamond has a small red rose tattooed on the left side of her neck," he replied, caressing the area in question with a feather of his fingertips.

A shudder shook through Jane at his warm touch. "I . . . I don't have a . . . a tattoo."

"I figured it was just a mistake on the wanted poster."

She smiled hesitantly. "Apparently not."

He curled his fingers around the back of her neck, still caressing with warm, light strokes. "Do you have any idea what you've done to me, Jane Baker?"

Jane's eyes rounded. "I'm so sorry, Mr. Kincaid. I really will do my very best to win this tournament, and—"

"I've fought like hell not to fall for you, thinking you were a heartless killer. But now . . . "

Jane blinked in surprise at his confession, and then was stunned to her toes when he leaned forward and kissed her deeply, passionately, pulling a gasp from her throat and all the air from her lungs. But she couldn't risk another heartbreak like she'd had the night before.

She pulled back from him, her erratic breathing making her dizzy to the point of needing to brace her hands against his chest once more. "What was that for?"

He tilted her face up to his. "Don't try to deny that you want me as much as I want you. I've felt it in every one of your sweet, warm kisses."

Jane certainly couldn't deny her desire for him; it was written all over in the hot blush staining her cheeks. "You want me?" she asked tremulously.

"Very, very much," he whispered almost painfully.

Before she could take another breath he was kissing her again. This time Jane slid her eyes closed and let the sensations of being held by him sink into her very being. He wanted her. Dolan Kincaid, handsome, powerful, incredible man that he was, wanted *her*.

And Jane knew she wanted him too by the insistent ache that began to spiral deep in her belly. He was holding her tightly, with a strength that made her feel both cherished and possessed, as he moved his mouth over hers and stoked the fire in her soul.

She suddenly couldn't seem to get close enough to him, to get enough of their reckless embrace. She moved restlessly, and he moaned deeply into her mouth. She wanted more, so much more.

But when he cupped her bottom in his big strong

hands and brought her hips against the evidence of his desire, she went as stiff as a two-by-four.

Dolan broke their kiss and nuzzled the side of her neck. "God, Jane, don't pull back from me again," he begged, his voice hoarse with need.

His touch felt so good, so incredibly right. Jane wanted more, more kisses, more caresses, but at the same time she was scared to the depths of her heart. She wasn't exactly experienced in the ways of love; what if she embarrassed herself—or worse, disappointed him? "I . . . I've never . . . never . . . "

He pulled back and gazed into her eyes. "You've never what?"

She smiled weakly. Would he find her less desirable once he knew the truth? "I've never exactly been with . . . a man." She shifted her focus to the buttons on the front of his shirt as a hot blush crawled up her neck. "I'm not exactly the kind of woman men usually want."

"And what kind of woman do they want?"

She shrugged. "Pretty."

Without comment, he turned her around to face the mirror above the dresser. "What do you see?"

Jane reluctantly stared at her reflection, and saw a tousle-haired woman with flushed cheeks and puffy lips. Dolan's hands were on her waist as he looked expectantly at her reflection from over her shoulder, but Jane didn't know what to say. "A mess," was the first thing that came to her mind.

"I see a gorgeous mane of dark gold hair framing a pair of sparkling green eyes. A perfect, dainty nose. Lush, soft lips. A sleek, graceful neck," he said, kissing her behind the ear. "Delicate shoulders. Full, beautiful breasts," he whispered seductively, cupping her breasts in his large hands. Jane leaned back against him as his hands traveled down her stomach. "A slender waist. Gently curving hips. Long, gorgeous legs."

He was cradling her hips, kissing her lavishly on the neck, and Jane was watching their reflection in wonderment. Through his eyes, she saw the woman he was describing, the woman she'd been all along. But her lack of confidence had made her hide herself, cower from the world, and never notice what she was overlooking.

She broke into a bright smile. And her eyes sparkled with confidence, giving a certain competent tilt to her chin. She looked strong, capable . . . worthy. And she also looked damn good with Dolan Kincaid standing behind her.

"You're gentle," Dolan whispered in her ear. "Intelligent. Sweet—oh so very sweet," he added with a sexy laugh while playfully nipping her neck. "You're feisty, fragile, sexy, beautiful—"

"*Beautiful*?" she whispered, breathless from his lavish seduction.

He met her eyes in her reflection. "Beautiful."

Jane smiled and turned in his arms. "Thank you," she said.

"For what?"

"For helping me find myself."

"Kiss me, sweet Jane," he whispered. "Kiss me some more."

She leaned up on her toes and his mouth closed over hers. Jane melted in his arms. All her life she'd longed for this kind of connection, this kind of feeling. Who would have ever thought she'd find it with a man living in the nineteenth century?

And then realization struck. Yes, she'd found love

here in the past with Dolan. But she wouldn't be staying to enjoy it.

He was working loose the buttons on the front of her dress, and she anticipated the feel of his warm hands on her bare skin, knowing they might only have a few hours left. Tears burned her eyes, and drifted down her cheeks to mingle with their kiss.

Dolan pulled back from her and wiped the moisture from her face with his thumbs. "Don't be afraid." He looked down into her eyes with warmth, passion, a gaze full of promise. "I won't hurt you, Jane. I promise."

He would have no say in the matter. Inevitably she would leave. And that would hurt more than anything he could ever do to her physically. Everything about Dolan Kincaid, right down to the determined set of his jaw, called to her. She never felt as complete as when she was being held in his arms. He made her feel whole. And he would be out of her life for good very soon.

"I'm not afraid," she whispered back. She kissed him with love, sadness, joy, and desperation, not caring what the consequences might be after that day. Only knowing that she needed him now.

He scooped her up into his arms and laid her down on the bed in a puddle of yellow gingham. Then he took off his jacket and stretched out beside her to finish unbuttoning her dress. "You're so beautiful," he said, caressing the skin he was slowly revealing.

He eased both of her sleeves down her arms, caressing her all the way. "You're like satin," he murmured, placing a tender kiss on her bare shoulder.

His warm, questing mouth moved along her neck and then lower, until he was kissing the bared valley between her breasts. And then Jane closed her eyes as for the first time in her life her breasts were bared to the hungry eyes of a man.

Silence filled the room, that and Jane's own ragged breathing. She knew he was staring at her, and her nipples tightened uncontrollably at the thought.

She slowly opened her eyes, and modesty made her bring her hands together in an attempt to cover herself. He blocked her efforts by catching her hands in his. "Let me look at you," he whispered.

And then he bent his head and captured one of her taut nipples in his lips.

Jane gasped in shock at the electrifying sensation that sent a wave of tingles sweeping through her stomach. Her back seemed to arch of its own accord, urging him to have more.

Dolan raised up and yanked his shirt off over his head without bothering to unbutton it. Jane vaguely registered the sound of his shoes hitting the floor as the rest of her dress was pulled down her hips, down her thighs, and tugged free of her feet. She was left naked, vulnerable, and trembling in his arms. But she wasn't cold. Oh, lord, she was far from cold as he began his incredibly delicious ministrations on her other sensitive breast.

A hot, tight knot was coiling in her abdomen. All sense of modesty seemed to be forgotten as she pressed her head back into the pillows beneath her and reveled in the feel of him suckling her. She felt as if he were drawing out her very soul.

He took his time, tugging and nibbling, until Jane began to twist restlessly on the bed. And then his kisses began to travel lower, to her waist, her hips, her stomach, and finally the nest of golden curls between her thighs. By this time Jane was too far gone on the tide of desire to care what intimate things he did—as long as he didn't stop. His tongue pressed against her moist, sensitive flesh, and she willingly opened her thighs.

A few moments later, with her fingers threaded through the thickness of Dolan's hair, she felt the first delicious tremors of ecstasy. He moaned against her as she succumbed to the vibrant throbbings of climax. She called out his name, held him to her, and tumbled into a sensual haze.

When Jane came back to reality she was still breathing hard. Dolan had risen above her, and was biting at her lips. She smiled in contentment and slipped her arms around his muscular bare shoulders. Her body was practically humming. "Are you ready for me, sweet Jane?" he whispered passionately.

Knowing what he meant, Jane raised her knees alongside his hips, allowing him to slip down between her thighs. He let out a deep groan as the hard tip of him snuggled intimately against her damp heat. And then the rigid length of him pressed into her core.

Jane clenched her muscles in response to the unexpected tight, filling sensation, and Dolan let out another deep groan. "Christ, so sweet," he whispered. "So very sweet."

He moved within her at a steady, rhythmic pace that made the wrought-iron bed frame squeak. But Jane was past caring if the entire world heard them making love.

She instinctively arched her hips, and he slipped into her even deeper. "Sweet heavens," she gasped.

He kissed her, pressing his body to hers as he continued to thrust in and out in a wild, primitive dance that soon had both of them reaching for more. Jane could feel it building again, that same sweet ache threading itself through her body. And she could sense the same tension building in the powerful man above her.

She watched his face, watched the emotions play over his features as he threw his head back and thrust deeply within her. He called out her name, "Jane," and Jane didn't think she'd ever heard a more heartwarming sound. And then her body broke loose again, tearing free of physical bonds and flying into a brighter dimension as she followed the man she loved into the sensual storm.

A few minutes later, as Jane's heartbeat returned to normal, Dolan rolled to his side and pulled her against his chest. Jane smiled to herself, as he traced tiny circles around her dusky nipple.

"The final round starts again in an hour," he said.

She groaned and snuggled more tightly against him. She didn't want to think about the tournament now. She didn't want to think about anything but the sweet love they'd just made.

"Listen to me." He pulled her on top of him, and she stretched herself out luxuriously over the firm, hard planes of his body. "I think you should forfeit."

She giggled at what she thought must be a joke. "Don't be silly," she said, toying with the dark hair on his chest.

"I think we should just call it quits right now, Jane. Before . . . before you get yourself hurt."

She lifted up onto her elbows, and blinked at him in surprise. Concern was shining bright and clear in his eyes. "You're serious. But what about your money?"

He took her face in his hands and pulled her toward him for a tender kiss. "Forget the money. We'll be fine without it."

"Forget the money!" she said, flabbergasted. "You don't think I can win, do you?"

"Jane, you're gonna be up against the cream of the crop, now. These men are skilled cardsharps. They're going to catch you if you cheat too flagrantly."

Well, she'd certainly like to see one of them stop the game and accuse her of using an angel to read her opponents' cards. But, knowing that Nelson was the last subject Dolan ever wanted to hear about, she decided to keep that little comment to herself. His scowling expression mirrored his concern, and it warmed Jane's heart that he was willing to give up so much money for the sake of her safety.

"Dolan Kincaid," she said, smiling confidently down at him. "For once, you're just going to have to trust me."

# 15

*Jane was still adjusting her hair* as she sat down hastily at the finalists' table. She and Dolan had made passionate love again, and she'd barely gotten back into her dress when a knock came at her door telling her that play would start in five minutes.

Dolan had walked her to the main dining hall, stealing quick kisses all along the way. And before leaving her at her table, he'd given her one last lingering embrace for good luck. There was no doubt about it, she was head over heels in love.

Jane couldn't even resist glancing his way as the racks of chips were being handed out to the players. He was seated at the spectators' bar, already sipping his first drink. He was nervous for her. But she was determined that she wouldn't let him down.

Each player would be starting the final round with two thousand dollars in chips. And as Jane was counting hers, Nelson appeared behind Mr. Richard Cole, who was sitting across the table from her.

The angel gave her a bland stare over the man's blond head. "Have a nice little roll about, did we?"

Jane's jaw dropped open, and a hot blush crept up her neck. Unable to respond to that inflammatory statement, she gave Nelson a chilly glare, one that made Mr. Cole arch a quizzical eyebrow at her.

"Mrs. Kincaid," the blond man said. "You're looking lovely this afternoon."

"I believe *ravished* is more the word," Nelson remarked.

Jane thanked Mr. Cole for his compliment and, once the man had returned his attention to his chips, gave Nelson a glare to rival the fires of hell.

Their dealer, a large man wearing a white shirt and black sleeve garters, sat down beside Mr. Cole and began shuffling the deck.

"Same rules apply as before," Mr. McIntire said, standing beside the dealer. "Minimum ante is one hundred dollars. There is no betting limit. There will be no breaks. The game will continue until we have a winner. Mr. Rogers," he said to the dealer, "you may begin."

Mr. Rogers set the deck in front of Richard Cole to cut, and then began dealing out the first round of cards. Jane arched her brows as she picked up a pair of queens, a ten of spades, a three of diamonds, and a four of hearts.

"Stop that!" Nelson snapped. "No reactions—no expressions. Did everything I drum into your head during the last game slip out your ears while you were tumbling about in bed with Mr. Kincaid?"

Jane gritted her teeth and drummed her fingernails on the table, an action that caught the eyes of every player around the table and pulled yet another disapproving frown from Nelson. She wasn't surprised that he'd chosen to berate her here, in front of others, where she couldn't defend herself . . .

"Barely known the man for four days," he was grumbling.

. . . but when this tournament was over, Jane was going to give her self-righteous, self-serving spiritual guide a good solid piece of her mind.

"This man, here, has a possible straight to the jack," Nelson told her about the man to her left. "Our Mr. Cole is holding a pair of fours." He moved around the table to the gentleman on Jane's right. "And over here . . . absolutely nothing. Mr. Haskell will either fold immediately or try to bluff his way through a few bids."

Just as Nelson predicted, Jake Haskell folded after drawing three cards. Jane drew an ace and another queen. That gave her three queens. She tossed in two one-hundred-dollar chips, and the man seated to her left folded. Now only Jane's three of a kind and Mr. Cole's pair of fours remained. The betting went back and forth for a while, but she ended up winning that hand, and eagerly gathered in her pot of over eight hundred dollars.

Her enthusiasm waned during the next two hands, however, when she was forced to fold before the bidding even started. But, with Nelson's invaluable help, she won the next five hands after that.

During it all she stole quick, clandestine glances at Dolan. He was watching anxiously from the sidelines, and winked at her every time she caught his eye. Nothing could have bolstered her courage more than that.

She was winning. And the fact that she was cheating

abominably didn't bother her the slightest bit. According to Nelson, all the players in the tournament were cheating. And, unlike the others, her cause was a noble one. She wasn't cheating for her own sake; she was trying to help the man she loved.

Three hours later Jane and Mr. Richard Cole were the only two players left at the table. The man was good, very good. Nelson claimed that he was cheating his way through just about every hand, that he had aces appearing out of nowhere. Richard Cole would be a hard man to beat, but Jane wasn't worried. She had Nelson.

And then a strange little woman suddenly appeared behind Mr. Cole, and Nelson's blue eyes flew open so wide they just about came out of his head. "Stella!" he exclaimed, instantly breaking out in a sweat.

The woman had dark hair and small features. Her angular face was pinched, and she had her arms crossed over an elegant gray suit jacket. Though not much taller than five feet, the woman looked like a force to be reckoned with. And apparently Nelson agreed. He was jittering and stammering up a storm.

"Nelson," the woman stated in a fierce, angry voice. "I will see you in my office *immediately!*"

With that, the woman vanished as quickly as she'd appeared, and Nelson gave Jane a frantic glance. "So sorry, Miss Baker," he said with a weak smile. "Duty calls."

And to Jane's absolute horror, her only hope of winning vanished right before her eyes, leaving her sitting there with a hand amounting to nothing.

She blinked at where her angel had been standing, and then she broke out in a cold sweat of her own. She glanced at Dolan. He looked even more concerned than usual, no doubt having noticed her sudden pallor.

"Mrs. Kincaid?" Mr. Cole said.

Jane quickly smiled at her opponent.

"It's your bid."

Once again Jane looked at her cards. Before he'd so ruthlessly abandoned her, Nelson had informed her that Mr. Cole was holding a pair of fours, a masterpiece compared to what Jane had in her hand.

She'd have to bluff.

She gave her opponent a casual smile and pushed a third of her chips out onto the center of the table. "I bet . . . eight thousand dollars."

The entire room let out an audible gasp. Mr. Cole would have to wager almost all of his money in order to match her bet. Surely he'd read her aggressive action as cool confidence, and decide to cut his losses.

Her opponent studied her for a moment, glanced at his hand, and then studied her some more. Then he pushed eight thousand dollars in chips into the center of the table. "Call," he said evenly.

Jane's heart sank. The man laid down his two fours, and then added another to the mix: he'd obviously palmed one at some point.

Her entire body felt on fire as Jane slowly laid down her hand of absolutely nothing. The crowd gasped in disappointment and surprise, and she didn't have the courage to even glance at Dolan as Mr. Cole smiled smugly and scooped up over sixteen thousand dollars in winnings. Jane could have cried in that moment, but she remembered Nelson's instructions and kept her emotions and her facial expressions carefully in check.

If she had any hope at all of beating Mr. Richard

Cole, it would have to be with the next hand—before he had the chance to palm any more cards. She had one final chance to pull this off. And she was on her own.

She anted up, and then had to make a conscious effort not to hold her breath as the next hand was dealt out. With a passive expression, she picked up the ace of spades . . . then the ten of spades . . . then the queen of spades . . . and then the jack of spades. And she prided herself on not batting an eyelash, even though she felt as if she were about to explode with excitement. She was a heartbeat away from a royal flush: an unbeatable hand.

*Please, God, please,* she prayed mentally as she lifted up the next card. All she needed was the king of spades. It was the two of hearts.

Her heart sank, but Jane slid the useless card casually in with the rest of her hand, and looked up to see if Mr. Cole were giving any signs of what he might be holding. Out of the forty-two cards still remaining in the deck, she needed only one. She needed a miracle.

Richard Cole asked for only one card, a sure sign that he was either holding something impressive in his hand or he was intending to bluff her to the bank. Jane, too, asked for a single card. One perfect little card.

It was dealt to her facedown, and her hand shook ever so slightly as she picked it up and slid it into her hand. No outward motion or expression betrayed the almost explosive lurch of her heart as she glanced down at the king of spades. Now if she could only convince Richard Cole to bet everything he had.

With an artful subtlety, she allowed a brief bit of dismay to flit across her face, the sort of slip that would have made Nelson furious. Her opponent dropped five yellow chips into the center of the table. "I bet five hundred."

A very high bet to start with. Mr. Cole was obviously very confident in either his hand or his acting skills.

Jane considered the wager, and tapped her nails lightly on the table. She gave her opponent a tremulous smile. "I . . . I do believe this day has gone on long enough, Mr. Cole." With shaking hands, she pushed her entire rack of chips, almost sixteen thousand dollars, into the center of the table. "We look like we're about even, so I'll bet everything I have against everything you have."

The crowd surrounding the main floor began whispering among themselves, and pressed closer. Jane resisted the urge to look over at Dolan. She couldn't afford the distraction.

Richard Cole studied her for a moment, and Jane kept her expression immobile but fidgeted visibly with the button placket on the front of her dress—a motion Richard Cole's sharp gaze latched onto before he quickly looked back at his hand.

Finally, her opponent smiled. "All right, Mrs. Kincaid. I'll see your wager." He pushed his entire bankroll into the center of the table. "It has been a long day." He laid his hand out on the table with a great flourish, and grinned broadly. "Straight flush," he said. He leaned back in his chair, folded his hands over his stomach, and tossed a victorious grin to his wife, who was standing on the sidelines.

Jane stared at his hand. And then at his smug smile. And then, with a flick of her wrist, she tossed out her cards.

Her royal flush settled in the center of the table in the midst of thirty-two thousand dollars in poker chips and a pregnant pause of expectant silence. Richard Cole blinked in astonishment, and then glared at her with a mixture of anger and suspicion as the crowd erupted in a great roar of shouts and applause.

"I protest!" Mr. Cole shouted, leaping up from his chair. The crowd fell silent. "The woman obviously cheated!"

Jane felt a strong pair of hands fall down upon her shoulders and looked up to find Dolan standing behind her, glaring at Richard Cole.

Mr. McIntire strode forward. "That's a very strong accusation, Mr. Cole."

"How else could she have beaten me!" Richard Cole demanded, his face turning a bright, brilliant red. "She's hiding cards in her petticoats!"

Mr. McIntire settled a heavy gaze on Jane, and a tight lump of fear rose up in her throat. Dolan squeezed her shoulders and she reached up to grasp his hand for moral support. "Mrs. Kincaid," Mr. McIntire said, "*have* you been stashing cards in your petticoats?"

Jane stood, calmly. The crowd gawked in surprise when she lifted the hem of her yellow dress past her knees. "I don't even *wear* petticoats."

The room burst into shocked laughter, as did Mr. McIntire.

"To be honest, Mr. Cole," Dolan spoke up as he slipped his arm around Jane's waist and eased her up against his side. "Me and a couple of my fellow spectators at the bar were a little surprised at how often you seemed to come up with pairs."

Richard Cole blinked, and gave Dolan an up-down glance. "What, sir, are you suggesting?"

"That maybe we should all take a good look at *your* petticoats."

"Come on, Mr. Cole," Mr. McIntire said. "The lady was kind enough to show us her lovely legs. Let's have a look inside that jacket." He reached toward the man but Richard Cole jerked away.

"I am insulted, sir," Mr. Cole said, pulling his lapels tightly over his chest. "Insulted that you would—"

A large armed guard came up behind the man and pulled his arms to his sides.

"I will offer you my deepest apologies, sir, *after* I have examined your jacket." Mr. McIntire once again reached toward Richard Cole's jacket and yanked aside the lapels. Sure enough, a two of diamonds fell to the floor.

At that point Mr. Cole's face went from beet red to downright pale.

"Oh Dicky!" his wife cried, rushing to his side.

"Over the side with him!" someone called out from the crowd.

"Yeah, over the side!"

And the crowd began chanting for both Richard and Janet Cole to be tossed overboard.

The guard took Richard Cole by the back of his gray jacket and began leading him to the door.

"Hold on," Dolan said, walking after them. "I believe there's the small matter of a thousand dollars that you still owe me."

Glowering, Richard Cole yanked his billfold out of his inside jacket pocket and slapped a thousand dollars in cash into Dolan's open hand.

"Thank you," Dolan said. He smiled at the security guard. "You may continue."

The crowd fell very quiet as the Coles were hauled out onto the deck. A few moments later a loud splash was heard, and then another. The crowd broke into cheers.

Dolan lifted Jane up into his arms and kissed her soundly on the mouth. "You're amazing," he shouted above the roar. "Amazing!"

"I told you to trust me!" Jane shouted back.

He grinned broadly at her. "I'm gonna have to start listening to you more often!"

"Can I have that in writing?"

"Jane Baker, you can have the goddamn moon if you want it!"

She threw back her head and laughed. She'd won. For the first time in her life, she hadn't backed down, and not only had she won a sizable amount of money for the man she loved, she'd won her own self-confidence as well.


Nelson's stepped cautiously into Stella's office and closed the door. "I know how this looks—"

"*Looks?!*" the woman screeched from where she stood behind her desk. "What in heaven's name do you think you're doing?!"

Nelson mopped at his sweaty brow. No matter how hard he'd tried to avoid it, it seemed his day of reckoning had finally come. He moved closer, hoping a little height advantage might calm Stella down. It didn't. The woman glared up at him with eyes like drilling laser beams. "A small mishap occurred not too long ago with Miss Baker—"

"A mishap is *never* small when it comes to you. I've learned *that* if nothing else since you came to work in my department."

"Madam, I assure you that I have done the very best I could. It's that woman you assigned me to. Miss Baker has become *completely* unreasonable. And now she's gone and *slept* with the cad. She's turned into a veritable wanton!"

"I believe, Nelson," Stella said, easing down into her chair, "that you had best start from the beginning."

"Yes, yes. Well, first of all Miss Baker went and got herself *killed*—"

"And I'm sure you had nothing at all to do with that."

"Madam, I assure you, I did not even have an interaction with the woman for twelve hours before the event."

Stella leaned forward in her chair with a hardened glare. "You *deserted* her?" she demanded.

"Well"—he cleared his throat nervously—"*deserted* is a rather harsh word. I'd say more that I . . . I offered her an opportunity . . . an opportunity to deal with life on her own for a short while." He smiled hesitantly, knowing he was only making things worse with every word he said.

"Uh huh," Stella said, pursing her lips.

"I have since been doing everything in my power to remedy the situation."

"Why wasn't I informed of the *situation* immediately after it occurred?"

"Well, I certainly didn't want to bother you with—"

"Stop the hogwash, Nelson; you simply didn't want me finding out what a *fiasco* you'd made of yet another client's life."

Nelson's shoulders drooped and he finally gave up the fight. "You're right!" he cried, dropping his forehead into his hands. "Oh, you're right! I admit it! I didn't want to get myself in trouble, and so I further jeopardized Miss Baker by attempting to correct the situation on my own. I'm sorry," he said with heartfelt regret. "So sorry. I have really botched things up this time."

"What, exactly, did you do?" Stella asked calmly.

"I'm not sure," he whined. "I simply called up Miss Baker's file on my monitor, instructed that she be restored to her correct temporal location, and—"

"Well, there's your problem."

"What? Where?"

"You restored her to her *correct* temporal location, Nelson. Her correct temporal location—the place where Miss Baker was supposed to be born—is the nineteenth century. We discussed that during our last meeting."

"Yes! Yes, that's right," Nelson said eagerly.

"Now tell me about this man she's succumbed to."

Nelson flashed his superior a look of distaste. "He's an uncouth, unwashed, uneducated brute. He's constantly grabbing, swearing, shooting—I don't know what she sees in him."

"Perhaps the other half of herself."

He gave her a quizzical look, not quite understanding her point.

"Nelson, when souls are sent to earth, they naturally migrate to their other half, their soul mate. Occasionally this process fails, as you well know, and clients can be born in the wrong year—or even the wrong century. This, again, was the case with Miss Baker. After much deliberation, it was decided that she did not have the wherewithal to survive nineteenth-century life, which is why her location was never remedied. But now you've sent her back to her correct temporal location, and this time, it seems, her soul has gotten it right. Dolan Kincaid is her soul mate."

"Good heavens! *That poor woman!*"

"I'm sure Miss Baker isn't counting herself poor at all. Thus the chances of you getting her to agree to leave now that she's met the man of her dreams are fairly slim."

"But she promised me she would go home once I figured out how to get her there without jumping her off a cliff," Nelson stated adamantly.

Stella held up her hand. "I don't even want to know what you mean by that. As for this promise, are you quite sure she agreed?"

"Absolutely. I wouldn't have gone along with her ridiculous card scheme otherwise."

"Something else I gather I don't want to know about," Stella said dryly. "Well, if she made you a promise then that's all there is to it."

"*It?*"

"Once they've agreed to a relocation, Nelson, it's merely a simple matter of making the correct arrangements."

For the first time in days, Nelson began to have some hope. "Then I haven't mucked things up permanently this time?"

"No. But you still have an awful lot to learn. Now, let's get Miss Jane Baker back where she belongs, back to where she'll be able to live out a safe, uncomplicated life."

Nelson smiled with relief. "Yes, *ma'am.*"

"And then," Stella added, leaning across her desk toward him, "I think I might just assign you to that hamster you've been speaking so highly of."

# 16

*Jane rode silently* along beside Dolan as they headed out of Sacramento with their saddlebags full of thirty-two thousand dollars in cash.

Dolan had been strangely quiet since they'd left the paddle wheeler, and Jane was feeling decidedly torn. She wanted to go home, back to good old 1997, where everything was comfortable and familiar; but another part of her, the part she suspected had been set free in the past four days, wanted to stay right where she was, in the nineteenth century with the man she loved.

"You ever been to Montana, Jane?" Dolan suddenly asked her.

She gave him a startled look. "No."

"Nothing but blue and green as far as the eye can see, and mountains frame every sunrise."

"It sounds beautiful."

They rode on in silence for a few minutes more. "You gonna be headin' south?" he asked.

"I suppose." Jane hadn't really considered what she'd

do once she and Dolan headed in separate directions. She supposed she hadn't wanted to think about it.

"Sounds like you don't have any definite plans."

"I guess I don't."

Suddenly he turned his horse in front of hers and pulled up short. "Listen . . ." He glanced up at the cloudless sky as if searching for the right words. "Could I interest you in coming north with me?"

Jane's heart nearly stopped. "With *you*?"

"There's four hundred acres of prime cattle land with my name on it just outside of Billings, and . . . well, I'd love to show it to you."

Jane couldn't believe her ears. He was asking her to go with him? And the funny thing was, he actually looked as if he were afraid she might say no.

She laughed nervously. "You want to show me a ranch?"

He sighed. "It's more than that. I . . ." He looked at her with so much raw emotion on his face that Jane almost burst into tears. "I don't wanna say good-bye."

Jane's throat tightened. "I don't want to say good-bye either."

He broke into a grin. "Well, then, what the hell are we doin'?"

"I don't know," Jane said, laughing. "Being stubborn, I guess."

"Something I hear I do very well."

"*No!*" Jane said dramatically. "Why, you're the most reasonable, open-minded man I know."

He laughed, and scooped her out of her saddle and onto his lap. He kissed her deeply, his mouth gliding over hers in an urgency that left Jane breathless. And in that moment she knew, instinctively, that she belonged in the nineteenth century in Dolan Kincaid's arms.

"I'm so glad fate made me stumble across you in that meadow, Jane," he said softly a few moments later.

Jane smiled and snuggled against his chest. The next time she saw Nelson she'd pass along Dolan's gratitude—right after she informed the angel that she'd changed her mind: She wouldn't be going home after all.

He came toward her with the moonlight reflecting off the water that lapped at his lean, hard body. They'd been on the trail for the past three hours, until it had grown too dark to see, and now the cold, clear water of the gently flowing river felt good against Jane's skin.

Despite the intimacies they'd shared only that afternoon, she crossed her arms over her chest as Dolan waded toward her from the shore. "I . . . I thought you were going to build a fire," she said.

He grinned, primitively, and continued toward her until she had to look up to see into his eyes. "I built one at the campsite. Now I thought I'd see what I could come up with out here in the water."

Jane's gaze traveled down the hard, muscular wall of his chest, over his abdomen, and to the faint line of dark hair that began at his navel and disappeared beneath the water. She wasn't sure what to say, how to act. She was just too new at this.

"Put your arms down, Jane," he commanded gently.

Jane swallowed her nervousness, and slowly lowered her arms. She couldn't look away as Dolan's gaze traveled over her face, down her shoulders, to her bare breasts. He dragged a finger over one of her taut nipples. "How'd I ever get so lucky?" he whispered, lowering himself to his knees in front of her.

He took her by the hips, and Jane gasped as he covered one of her nipples with his mouth and nipped at it with his teeth. He gently coaxed her into straddling his thighs, and sat down with her in the cool water. He kissed her, slow and deep, and Jane let out a soft moan as he lifted her by the waist and slipped his hard, steely flesh inside her.

She locked her legs around his hips, and kissed him passionately as they rocked back and forth with the water lapping at their bodies. She cried out as a climax overtook her, shouting his name to the night sky, and reveled in the feeling of him surging within her.

Afterward, they dried each other off, dressed, and snuggled down in their shared bedroll by the fire. If this was what life would be like with the man she loved, then Jane couldn't wait to get started. She fell asleep in his arms, snuggling warmly against his chest, and lulled into peacefulness by the steady rhythm of his heartbeat.

Some hours later, both Jane and Dolan were startled awake by a loud shout.

"Holy sakes alive!"

They both bolted upright. Their fire had gone out, leaving their campsite in relative darkness. But it wasn't too dark to make out the shapes of Barney Rollins and Cleavus Coltrain. It was Cleavus who had shouted. The two men were standing by their horses only a few feet away, and their jaws were hanging open in shock.

"Miss Rose!" Cleavus shouted excitedly. "We thought they hung ya in Sacramento yesterday!"

Dolan groaned, and rubbed the sleep from his eyes. "Look, you idiots, this is not Rose Diamond. This is Jane Baker."

The men gave him a dark stare. "You ain't gonna pull one over on us, Kincaid. That there is Miss Rose. I know her as well as I know the back of my hand."

"You're gonna know the back of mine if you don't get the hell back on your horse and ride the hell on."

"We're so glad to see you're all right, Miss Rose," Cleavus said, ignoring Dolan's threat. "When we got word that you'd been hanged, well . . . we darn near died o' grief ourselves."

"Goddamn it," Dolan shouted. "She isn't—"

Jane turned to Dolan and pressed her fingers to his lips. "Let me handle this." She smiled at the two men who were so intent on rescuing her. "Listen, fellas, plans have changed. I've decided to stay with Mr. Kincaid, indefinitely."

Cleavus and Barney looked at her as if she'd lost her mind.

Jane shrugged, and looked at Dolan. "I've fallen in love with him."

Dolan smiled warmly at her, and reached out to stroke the side of her face.

"Ah, Miss Rose," Barney said with a grimace. "Say it ain't so."

"Does that mean we gotta do what *he* says now?" Cleavus whispered to his partner.

"Shh!" Barney hissed. "Lemme think!"

"Everybody stand back," Dolan said dryly.

And then Nelson suddenly popped into view. "Good evening, Miss Baker."

"What is this," Jane grumbled, "a party?"

"There is something I need to discuss with you," Nelson continued.

"There's something I need to discuss with you too," Jane said. Dolan gave her an odd look, and she flashed him a smile. "But not now," she added through her teeth. She turned her attention back to Barney and Cleavus. "So, you see, gentlemen, I don't need you to rescue me. I'm happy right here." She gave Nelson a direct look. *"With Dolan."*

"Listen," Dolan said, "you boys ride on out of here now, and I'll forget the past few days ever even happened."

"We're not goin' anywhere without Miss Rose!" Barney shouted.

"Yeah!" Cleavus agreed.

Barney slid his gun out of his holster and aimed it right at Dolan. "You've obviously put some kinda spell on her. Don't worry, Miss Rose, we won't leave without ya."

Nelson cleared his throat. "Miss Baker. Really. I *must* speak with you."

Jane ignored him. She was too intent on the gun in Barney's hand. "Barney. Don't be ridiculous. Put that gun away."

"Damn it, Barney!" Dolan shouted. "She's not Rose! And the lady isn't interested in being rescued anymore!"

But Barney wasn't listening. With a shaking hand, he cocked his gun. "I'm gonna count to three, Kincaid. And if you haven't moved away from her by then, I'm . . . well . . . I'm gonna shoot ya. One."

"Dolan, move away," Jane said.

"For Christ's sake, Jane. The man couldn't shoot *himself* if he tried."

"Two."

But there was something in Barney Rollins's eyes, some glint of determination that frightened Jane. It was obvious that the news of Rose's death had seriously rattled him.

"Dolan," she warned.

"Three," Barney announced. He squeezed his eyes closed and pulled the trigger on his gun.

The shot rang through the air, and Jane let out a scream that echoed off the water nearby. She felt a sharp, sudden burning sensation in her chest, and found it suddenly difficult to breathe.

"Sweet Jesus," Dolan gasped. "Oh God— *Jane!*"

"What's happened?" Jane said, suddenly feeling weak.

She looked down at her chest, and saw a rapidly spreading dark stain on the front of her yellow dress. Sharp needles of pain shot through her back, and then her legs went numb.

She fell against Dolan's chest and he gently lowered her to the ground. He did his best to stanch the bleeding with her blanket as Barney and Cleavus hovered over her, but Jane knew his efforts weren't doing any good. She could feel the life draining out of her.

There were tears in Dolan's eyes. "You're gonna be okay, Jane. Everything will be okay." He was rocking her gently. "Oh, sweetheart. I love you. I love you."

But Jane could see Nelson standing above her. And she knew that everything wasn't going to be all right. Whether she wanted it or not, she was being sent home.

Tears blurred her vision.

Barney was shaking his head. "I didn't mean it. I didn't mean it, Miss Rose."

Jane tried to speak, but couldn't. The numbness in her legs had spread upward to her stomach, then to her chest, and was now settling in her neck. She looked past Dolan's shoulder and gave Nelson a desperate, pleading stare. She didn't want this! She wanted to stay!

"I tried to tell you, Miss Baker," Nelson said gently. "It is time for you to go."

Jane looked frantically at Dolan. His own pain sank into her breaking heart. How could she go back to her old life when everything she wanted, everything she loved was right here?

"I love you," Dolan leaned close to whisper. He kissed her sweetly, and she tasted the salt of his tears. "I love you, Jane."

Jane struggled against the inevitable, focusing on his face as best she could, until she could no longer keep her eyes open. And then a bright, warm light appeared above her in the night sky, and began drawing her toward it. It was warm and accepting, but she resisted it until she'd used up every last drop of her remaining strength. And then it pulled her in, away from her body.

And as Jane floated upward, toward a life she didn't want, a century she didn't fit into, in her ears echoed the soft, muffled sobs of the man she was leaving behind.

# 17

*Jane sat up in her bed with a start.* Disoriented, she glanced around her room at her white dresser, her floral wallpaper, and her cushioned rocking chair in the far corner. She was home.

"*No!!*" she cried, throwing back her covers. She rose to her knees in the middle of her bed. "I don't want to be here! I wanted to stay with Dolan!"

She'd finally found love—real, true love, and it had been ripped from her hands like an undeserved gift.

Pain filled her heart, an ache so deep that she thought she might die all over again. How could she go on without Dolan in her life?

"I'm sorry, Miss Baker."

Jane turned her tear-filled eyes to where Nelson suddenly stood at the foot of her bed. "There's been a mistake," she said, emotion choking her voice. "You have to send me back."

"I can't do that."

"Why?" she cried. "Why can't I be with him?"

"Because this is where you belong," Nelson said gently.

"I *don't* belong here!" she said angrily. "I've *never* belonged here! Oh Nelson, I feel as if someone has just cut me in half."

"Please, Miss Baker, forgive me. Forgive me for doing this to you. I am so very sorry."

"Forgive you? For what? For ripping love out of my hands after I'd spent my whole life searching for it?"

"This has all been a very unfortunate tragedy."

Jane sniffled, and wiped the dampness from her face. "So what am I supposed to do now? Go on with my life as if nothing happened? As if the man I love hasn't"—a new sob caught in her chest—"hasn't been dead and buried for years? Tell me how I do that, Nelson!"

"I . . ." He looked down at the floor. "I don't know."

"Some guardian angel you turned out to be!" she shouted bitterly. "But what other kind would they assign to poor, pathetic Jane Baker, except an inept one?"

"I, um, I requested that you be returned home the weekend before you left, so you could have a few days to pull yourself together. It's early Saturday morning. The thirty-first of May."

"How very thoughtful of you. Unfortunately I think it's going to take more than a quiet weekend to get over what's happened to me."

"Miss Baker, I did the very best I could—"

"Well, it wasn't good enough, was it, Nelson!"

"I understand. I'll leave you alone now." And he slowly faded from sight.

Jane stared at the empty room as emotions continued to build within her like a gathering storm. She lowered her face into her hands and broke into wrenching sobs that felt as if they would tear her in two. If living meant being without Dolan, then she didn't want to live at all.

His mind made up, and his courage gathered firmly around him, Nelson strode into Stella's office without bothering to knock. "Madam, I would have a word with you."

Stella glanced up from what she was reading and frowned at him. "What is it now, Nelson? Don't tell me you've managed to kill your hamster."

Nelson took a deep breath and thrust out his chin. "Stella, I request—no, no, I *demand* another hearing."

The woman blinked. "A hearing? A hearing for whom? At last count, I believe you were fresh out of clients."

"Another hearing for Miss Jane Baker. The woman is completely beside herself with grief."

Stella gave him an arch look. "And whose fault is that?"

"Mine. Her heartache is completely my fault. And I fully intend to do everything in my power to rectify the matter."

Stella leaned back in her chair. "Nelson, as I told you, a hearing *was* held for Miss Baker. And it was determined that she was incapable of surviving in the nineteenth—"

"Yes, yes, I already know all that. But things have changed. I believe my client has proven herself very capable indeed. And I *demand* the opportunity to prove it."

"Well, well. It seems the woman is capable of many things, including taking the starch out of one rather haughty angel."

"Miss Baker is a very remarkable woman. Capable of much more than she has ever given herself credit for."

Stella considered him for a moment, and Nelson held his breath. "All right," she finally said. "I'll schedule a new hearing as soon as possible."

Nelson sighed in audible relief.

"But be forewarned," she added. "This task won't be easy. A decision not to relocate is never made lightly, and one has *never* been overturned."

"Well then, madam," Nelson said, smiling smugly, "you may consider history made."


Jane sat in bed for two days, not eating, not sleeping, not even caring. She supposed a part of her actually hoped that she could just waste away, leave this earth before she had to spend one more minute without Dolan.

But by early Monday morning her mind had cleared a bit, and she was thinking more rationally. Yes, life would be painful and lonely without the man she loved. But if she'd learned anything at all during her stay in the nineteenth century it was that she was capable of surviving just about anything.

She was stronger than she'd ever given herself credit for. That was why Dolan had fallen in love with her. And she wasn't going to let him—or herself—down by quitting now.

She rose from her bed and padded to her closet in her bare feet and nightgown. She stared at the white skirt hanging there, spotless, as it had been before she'd put it on that momentous morning less than a week ago. She passed it by for a simple pair of jeans, and a plain white

T-shirt. She'd never gone to work dressed in anything but skirts. But she wasn't about to start living her life in the pathetic manner in which she had before.

Once dressed, she went through the motions of brushing her teeth and hair, and making herself a strong cup of coffee. Absently she left the house and walked the three blocks to the library; she was ten minutes late in opening the double glass doors. But she didn't care. She'd learned that life had more meaning than punctuality and precision.

She was amazed that everything in the twentieth century could still be the same when she was so very different. She ran her fingers along the top of her white work counter, and sat down on the black vinyl stool. And with less than enthusiastic work ethic, she began organizing the books that had been left in the drop box over the weekend.

The day progressed much the same as it had before, only this time Jane was uninvolved. Her heart, her mind, was in another time, another place. Everyone that came in paused and stared at her as if she'd grown a third eye, but Jane didn't care to explain her transformation.

The two teenagers strolled into the library around two o'clock, and began tearing the suggestive pages out of a romance novel. And again, Jane didn't care. The place could have burned down around her ears and she would have simply shrugged and headed home for the day.

And then Paula Preston came strolling into the library. She leaned across Jane's work counter and popped her gum in her face.

"Hot date with a casting director last night?" Jane asked, not looking up from the books she was stamping.

"I guess good news travels fast," Paula replied smugly.

"Guess so."

"He's going to be—"

"Casting the Sylvester Stallone movie?"

"That's right." Paula pressed her large breasts into Jane's line of vision. "Just think, you might get to see these smashed against Sly's tanned chest in a movie soon."

Impatient with this scene that she'd already played out before, Jane smiled tightly at her. "How marvelous."

Paula gave her an odd look. "Say, did you get your hair cut?"

"No." Jane just hadn't bothered to pull it back into her usual tight ponytail.

Paula's smile returned. "Well, don't be jealous, Plain Jane, I mean about Sly and me. Someday your ship will come in. It'll be small, and rotted, and full of holes, but it'll come in."

"Uh huh. Listen, Paula?" Jane began with a dramatic frown. "If you don't get those things off my work counter and out of my face, I'm gonna hack 'em off with a butter knife."

Paula blinked in surprise, and moved back a step. "Sheesh. What's up your butt today?"

"What, exactly, do you want?"

"I'm here for a book."

"Right," Jane said, stamping another due date. "One on sharks."

"No, one on fishing," Paula replied snidely, apparently pleased that Jane had finally gotten something wrong.

"Because the *movie* is about a loan shark."

"Right," Paula replied, and snapped her gum.

"You'll find what you're looking for at the top of the third shelf from the door."

"Where'd you get that tan, Janey? God, I hope you haven't been lying out in a string bikini and scaring all your neighbors."

"At least I could fit into a string bikini, honey. I doubt you could leash those two babies down with steel plates and a mile of duct tape."

Paula's splayed hand suddenly appeared in the spot that Jane was about to stamp. "I don't know what you're on, Plain Jane, but you are walkin' a thin line, here."

Jane looked up and smiled at Paula Preston. She calmly set her stamper down on the countertop. After thirty years, she'd had enough.

She reached out, took a fistful of bleached blond hair, and spiked Paula Preston's face down onto her sticky red ink pad.

Paula let out a shriek, and lurched upright, her mouth open, her hands held out as if she'd been drenched with acid. She had a red nose, a red cheek, a scarlet right eye, and one long, crimson strand of hair hung limply, tauntingly in her face. "You little bitch!" she shouted. "Look what you did!"

"I thought you could use a little more color," Jane said, circling her work counter. She took Paula by the arm and dragged her toward the double glass doors. "And now, it's time to put out the trash."

"But what about my book!" Paula shouted.

"We have several criteria when it comes to checking out books in the library, Miss Preston," Jane said, pushing open the double glass doors. "And literacy happens to be at the top of the list." With that, Jane gave Paula a shove that sent the woman stumbling outside.

Jane closed the library a half hour early that day, although she had nothing to go home to but an empty house. She'd somehow managed to make it through one full day without Dolan, but she wondered how in the world she was going to make it through tomorrow. And the tomorrow after that.

She took a shower and made herself a single entrée in the microwave. Then she sat down in front of her television set and tried to become caught up in a dramatic movie of the week, but her mind wandered so often that within thirty minutes she had no idea what was going on. She shut off the television and went out into her backyard for some fresh air.

The night sky was full of stars, and the moon was a crescent above her head. She wondered how many times Dolan had looked up at that sky and thought of her during his lifetime. Had he been happy without her?

She walked to the chestnut tree by the back fence and sat down on the grass to lean up against its thick trunk. Its branches blocked the sky and sheltered her in comforting darkness. She would survive. She had to. And then, one day, they'd be together again.

# Epilogue

*A bird singing above her head* pulled Jane awake the next morning. She opened her eyes into the bright sun and stared up at a cloudless sky. She wondered what time it was. She needed to open the library. And then she frowned in confusion. She suddenly realized that her fence was missing. In fact, nothing around her looked familiar.

"Are you all right?"

She started, and looked up at a very pregnant blond woman. "I . . . I fell asleep."

"I know. I didn't have the heart to wake you. From what I've heard you've had a pretty rough week."

Jane stared up at the woman in confusion. "Are you . . . my new spiritual guide? Where"—she looked around—"where am I now?"

The woman gave her a surprised look. "You're, um, you're in Pine Oaks, Jane. Staying with me and Jack. Remember? Kristen and Jack Ford?"

"Jack Ford? The marshal Jack Ford?" Jane slowly rose to her feet and brushed off the back of her jeans.

"That's right. Hey, it's nice to see my old clothes fit you. I hope they fit me again eventually," she added, patting her expanded belly.

Jane glanced down at the jeans and T-shirt she was wearing. "Your clothes?"

"Jane, are you all right? You seem a little confused. Maybe I should go get Dolan."

Jane's heart lurched. "Dolan? Dolan's *here*?"

"Of course he's here. He and Jack are out in back of the house fixing the chicken coop."

Jane didn't even let Kristen Ford finish speaking before turning and running toward the house a few yards away. When she saw the familiar shape of the man she loved crouched down beside the marshal of Pine Oaks, tears filled her eyes. She stopped, out of breath, at the split-rail fence. "Dolan!" she cried.

He stood and turned toward her, smiling that crooked smile of his, and her heart filled with so much love and joy she thought it might burst. She hurdled the fence, and threw herself into his arms.

"What's the matter, sweetheart?" he asked, concern deepening his voice. He held her tightly, and Jane prayed with everything she had that he would never let her go.

She pulled back and looked into his handsome face. "I love you. I love you so much."

He smiled, and brushed away the tears streaming down her cheeks. "What are all these tears about?"

"I was afraid . . . I'd lost you."

"She fell asleep in the meadow," Kristen Ford said. She'd finally managed to catch up to Jane. "I think she might have had a bad dream."

"Barney Rollins shot me last night, Dolan." Jane put

her hand over the spot where the bullet had pierced her chest. "He shot me. Right here. I died—I left you!"

Dolan cupped her face in his hands and kissed her tenderly. "It was a just a dream, Jane," he whispered. "We spent last night safe and warm in each other's arms. Now that Rose Diamond is gone, I'm sure we've seen the last of Barney and Cleavus."

With a relieved sob, Jane threw her arms around his neck. She was back. She was home.

"Happy, Miss Baker?"

She looked up, past Dolan's shoulder, and saw Nelson standing by the chicken coop. His Italian leather loafers were, of course, poised above the muck and mud.

"You're where you belong now," he added with a warm smile. "With your soul mate."

"Thank you," Jane whispered, filled with so many emotions she could barely speak. "Thank you so much."

"You, Miss Baker, are very welcome." Nelson smiled at her one last time and slowly faded away.

"Thank me for what?" Dolan said, pulling back to smile into her face.

She smiled back at the man she loved. "For loving me, Dolan Kincaid."

Jack Ford, the marshal of Pine Oaks, opened a gate and helped his pregnant wife into the yard. "I think what the two of 'em need is a healthy meal and a good night's sleep," he said to his wife.

"Sounds good to me," Dolan said. He wrapped his arm around Jane's waist and began leading her toward the house.

"Any preferences?" Kristen asked, as they all stepped up onto the back porch. "You better call it now, Jane, or Dolan'll be demanding chicken and dumplings."

"Just a simple hamburger sounds good to me," Jane replied, tearing her gaze away from Dolan.

Kristen gave her a speculative look. Then she broke into what could only be described as a secretive smile and leaned closer to Jane. "Would you like special sauce, lettuce, cheese, pickles, onions, and a sesame seed bun with that?"

Jane stared at her in shock. And then the two of them broke into laughter as the men they loved looked on in baffled amusement.